Readers love And

Accompanied by a Waltz

"A story about first love, loss, and the rediscovery of love all wrapped up in its pages."
—Fallen Angel Reviews

A Serving of Love

"…a compelling tale of two men who meet under less than favorable conditions and find something that is well worth the effort."
—Sensual Reads

Dutch Treat

"The emotional pull was strong and the story was great It was definitely worth reading, and will become a permanent addition to my library for sure."
—Long and Short Reviews (formerly Whipped Cream Reviews)

Positive Resistance

"With the right amount of suspense, sizzle and a burgeoning romance between two people, the readers are treated to a story that hits all the right spots in your heart."
—Love Romances & More

Love Means… No Fear

"I would recommend this story to anyone looking for romance. I also found this series to be a lovely introduction to m/m erotica."
—The Romance Studio

http://www.dreamspinnerpress.com

Novels by
ANDREW GREY

Accompanied by a Waltz
Dutch Treat
Seven Days
Work Me Out (anthology)

THE ART STORIES
Legal Artistry
Artistic Appeal
Artistic Pursuits
Legal Tender

THE BOTTLED UP STORIES
Bottled Up
Uncorked
The Best Revenge
An Unexpected Vintage

THE CHILDREN OF BACCHUS STORIES
Children of Bacchus
Thursday's Child
Child of Joy

THE LOVE MEANS… STORIES
Love Means… No Shame
Love Means… Courage
Love Means… No Boundaries
Love Means… Freedom
Love Means … No Fear
Love Means… Healing
Love Means… Family

THE RANGE STORIES
A Shared Range
A Troubled Range
An Unsettled Range

THE TASTE OF LOVE STORIES
A Taste of Love
A Serving of Love
A Helping of Love

All published by
DREAMSPINNER PRESS

LEGAL TENDER

ANDREW GREY

Dreamspinner Press

Published by
Dreamspinner Press
382 NE 191st Street #88329
Miami, FL 33179-3899, USA
http://www.dreamspinnerpress.com/

Legal Tender

Cover Art by Anne Cain   annecain.art@gmail.com
Cover Design by Mara McKennen

ISBN: 978-1-61372-437-8

Printed in the United States of America
First Edition
April 2012

eBook edition available
eBook ISBN: 978-1-61372-438-5

To my nieces, Sofia and Vivian.
I hope someday you'll read my stories.

PROLOGUE

TIMOTHY BESCH pulled his old clunker of a car into the parking lot of the nursing home on Milwaukee's East Side, hoping the old thing would make it for just a few more months. Every now and then it made a sound like gunfire, and it chose that moment to do it. Letting off the gas, he glided into a parking space and turned the key. The engine ran for a few seconds before finally dying. Every time that happened, Timothy wondered if that would be the end and the old thing would give up the ghost. Not that he could blame it.

His car door groaned, metal scraping metal as he opened the driver's door and stepped out of what he knew was probably a death trap, but for now he had no choice. Another car was not a priority. He had less than six months to go and he would actually graduate from college—with a mountain of debt, but he would graduate. Timothy closed the door, getting an even louder than normal screech of protest, walked toward the front door, and went inside.

The place was depressing; it always had been. And it wasn't just because it was a nursing home, but one of those that took people who had nowhere else to go. Timothy hated it and wanted so badly to move Grampy to another place, but his grandfather wouldn't hear of it. Walking down the hallway, he passed old men and women sitting in wheelchairs, moving slowly down the halls like they were pulling the entire weight of their own lives behind them. Wrinkled faces looked up at him like puppy dogs begging for a little attention. As he walked, Timothy said good morning to everyone who met his eyes. Some he knew by name, some he didn't, but it didn't matter to them or him. One lady reached to him, taking Timothy's hand in hers. Rose was always a breath of fresh air in this dreary place. Eyes bright, sharp as a tack, hands curled with arthritis, and nearly deaf, she put her skinny arms around his neck, pulling him into a hug the way she always did. Timothy relished this simple gesture every time he visited, probably because they both needed the simple contact and comfort. "I'll come to visit with you once I see Grampy," Timothy promised, as he always did. After visiting Grampy, he always stopped to see Rose for a few minutes. She nodded, knowing the routine, and Timothy continued down the hall.

"Hi, Grampy," Timothy said with as much of a smile as he could muster as he walked into the small room. At least Grampy had his own room instead of sharing with someone else. Timothy saw Grampy's eyes open, and the elderly man smiled a little bit. He was so weak lately, but Grampy tried to sit up, and Timothy helped by propping pillows behind him.

"How are you feeling?" Timothy sat in the chair next to the bed, holding Grampy's hand. He used to hug him, but Grampy had become so fragile, and his skin so sensitive, that additional stimulation hurt. So Timothy contented both of them by holding his hand.

"My legs itch," Grampy said, and Timothy looked down at the bedding, to where Grampy's legs would have been if he still had them. His circulation had stopped, and they'd had to amputate over a year ago. He'd gotten better at first and was more alert after the surgery, but since then, he'd slowly returned to what he was like before his legs were taken. Timothy often wondered if they simply should have let Grampy die, but he hadn't been able to bear that thought, so he'd made the toughest decision of his young life and let the doctors take Grampy's legs. Now he wondered constantly if he'd made the right decision.

"I know," Timothy said. "Close your eyes, and I'll scratch them for you." Timothy had been told that these were phantoms. Timothy made scratching sounds on the bed, and Grampy sighed softly, like he was feeling better. It was all in Grampy's mind, so Timothy played along, and Grampy felt better. "Has anyone been up to see you?"

"Your mother was here yesterday," Grampy said softly. "She wanted money, and I told her to get a job." Grampy smiled and laughed a little. "She always was a lazy thing." Timothy agreed with him but kept quiet. There was no need to upset him, and at least Grampy hadn't given her any money. "I saved it all for you, Timmy," Grampy added. "All I had I saved for you."

"Grampy, you don't need to save anything for me. You need it for you," Timothy said, but Grampy had his eyes closed, and he was no longer with him. Their visits often went like this. When Grampy got tired, his mind would wander and he wouldn't make much sense.

"I saved it for you, Timmy. I put it where you always played." Grampy muttered something else and sat back in the bed, holding his hand like he had before. "The nurse came in here yesterday, and she had a banana on her head." Grampy's eyes shot open, and he turned his head toward Timothy. "Who are you?"

"I'm Timothy, Grampy. Remember?" Sometimes he did and sometimes he didn't. The moments of lucidity were unfortunately becoming fewer and fewer. "Go to sleep. I'll sit with you for a while."

He shook his head on the pillow. "Remember the stories, Timmy. I can't give you much, but it's all in the stories. Tell me you remember the stories."

Timothy smiled. "I remember every one you ever told me." Timothy settled back in the chair. "You used to tell me all kinds of stories. We'd sit on the porch swing, and you would hold me on your lap and tell me about the things you and your dad did. Do you remember?" Grampy closed his eyes, and Timothy sat with him until he fell asleep.

"Remember the stories, Timmy," Grampy mumbled when Timothy got up to leave. "They're where you used to play."

"I will; I promise." Timothy patted Grampy's hand and left the room. He stopped at the nurse's station on his way out to make sure they checked on Grampy. Then he made his way to Rose's room and found her sitting in her chair in front of her small television with a pair of huge headphones on. She was watching the news, and as he entered, he heard her make a very unladylike noise.

He walked around the bed and touched her shoulder. She jumped a little before pulling off the headphones. "There you are. I thought you forgot me." She smiled, as if to say she really hadn't, and rolled back from the television after turning it off.

"I just stopped by to say hello. You don't have to stop watching because of me," Timothy explained.

She made the same sound as she had earlier. "The president was making a speech. That Bush kid is as dumb as a box of rocks." She actually made a hand gesture at the television before turning back to Timothy with a smile on her face. "I have some cookies here somewhere," she said, and Timothy smiled. She was always trying to feed him.

"So how are you doing today?"

"As good as I can be," she answered. "They have me making baby quilts." She rolled her old eyes as best she could. "There isn't a baby within ten miles of this place, and if there were, all these old folks would suck the life out of it. But I spend my days making baby quilts."

"It keeps you busy," Timothy said, sitting in the chair in the corner.

"Yes, I suppose they figure if they keep us busy, the inmates won't try to take over the asylum." They both laughed. Rose was a sharp cookie. She'd told him once that she was ninety-seven, and Timothy supposed at that age, she was entitled to say whatever she wanted. "How's your Grampy?"

"Not good," Timothy answered, and Rose nodded.

"This place isn't good for anybody. It's where they put us out of sight to die." She said it so matter-of-factly it seemed sort of shocking to Timothy, and he looked at his shoes, feeling lower than dirt that he couldn't find a better place for Grampy. "Hey, I didn't mean you. Your Grampy and I are the lucky ones." Her hand touched his leg reassuringly. "The kids visit me all the time, and you see your Grampy plenty. We aren't forgotten, but most of them are."

"But if I could find him a better place…," Timothy began, and Rose clucked her teeth.

"It isn't the place, because they're all the same. No matter how much you pay, it's still a home where you can be forgotten," Rose explained. "Sometimes the depression here is enough to suck the life out of you."

Timothy got up as two teenagers walked into the room, smiling and filled with energy. He said goodbye and left the room so Rose could visit with the kids. As he reached for the door, he heard all three of them laughing. Walking back down the hall, Timothy looked in on Grampy, who looked sound asleep. But he was playing possum, and as soon as he realized Timothy was there, he opened his eyes and tried to sit up. Timothy went back into the room and proceeded to have nearly the exact same visit he'd had less than an hour earlier, Grampy not remembering a thing. When he left a second time, Grampy said in a raised voice, "Remember the stories, Timmy."

Timothy hurried back into the room and hugged his Grampy. He knew he shouldn't, but he needed him so badly, and he felt Grampy's arms around him and heard him whispering nonsense into his ears. "I love you, Grampy."

"I love you too, Timmy," he said, barely above a whisper. When Timothy let go, Grampy closed his eyes once again but looked happier, and Timothy's spirit felt much lighter as he left the nursing home.

CHAPTER 1

TIMOTHY pulled his new car, the first he'd ever had, in front of what in his own mind he referred to as the house of horrors. Parking the car, Timothy tried to decide if he actually wanted to stop at all. He could simply pull away again and tell the lawyer to sell it, or better yet, bulldoze the place to the ground. But he knew he wouldn't do that. There were good memories here, too, but bad ones had been laid down on top of those, and they were the ones that were hard to forget, the ones he saw again and again in his dreams. The house had been Grampy's, and for that reason alone it held a place in his heart, but Grampy hadn't actually lived there for quite a while. And even when Grampy had, he couldn't stop the hurt. Getting out of the car, Timothy stared at the front door but didn't move.

"Timmy!" A familiar voice rang out, and he turned to see Dieter running toward him. They'd met when Timothy and his mother had first moved in with Grampy. Dieter nearly tackled him with his energetic hug. "Are you okay? I saw people evicting your mom, and I figured I wouldn't see you again." Dieter seemed so happy, and his energy dispelled some of the gloom Timothy was feeling.

"Well," Timothy began, wondering if Dieter would understand, "I was the one who tossed the deadbeats out on their sorry asses."

"You evicted your own mother?" Dieter stared at him openmouthed.

"Yup, and I would have done it years ago if I'd known Grampy had put the house in my name." Timothy felt the hate and rage swell inside him. "She's an addict who couldn't even show up for Grampy's funeral. I always thought Grampy had given her the house, that's what she said, but it was deeded to me years ago because he knew how my mother was." Dieter still stared at him with his mouth hanging open. "I know it sounds harsh, but the bitch hit Grampy before we got him in the nursing home," Timothy said. He didn't tell Dieter that she and sometimes her "boyfriends" had hit him too.

"Then good for you," Dieter said, and he put his arm around Timothy's shoulder like he'd done when they were kids. "I loved your Grampy. Do you remember the stories he used to tell?"

"All the time," Timothy said. "Do you still live in the same house?"

"Yeah. Gram died a while ago, and my partner Gerald and I live there now. Do you remember Tyler?" Dieter asked as they walked across the yard, and Timothy nodded. Tyler was older, so they weren't close friends. "He and his partner Mark bought his grandmother's house a while ago. It's like when we were kids, except the kids have taken over." Dieter snickered, the way Timothy remembered from when they were young, familiar and comforting in its way. "Are you going to keep the house?"

"I haven't decided. Mom didn't take good care of the place. But it was Grampy's house, and he'd hate to see it the way it looks now." Actually, the peeling paint and jungle yard would have broken Grampy's heart; Timothy knew it.

"Come on, let's take a look inside," Dieter said, and Timothy agreed. After all, that was why he was here, and at least he wouldn't have to see the mess on his own.

The inside wasn't as bad as he feared. It was mostly dirty and old. His mother, the old bitch, hadn't done anything, but at least she hadn't really damaged the place, either. "It needs a good cleaning and some paint," Timothy said as he walked from room to room. There was stuff piled in some of the corners and some old furniture. As he wandered around, he remembered these rooms when Grampy was still living here. The wallpaper in the living room was the same he remembered, faded with time, but still there.

"This is a great house. You could clean up the inside and have the outside painted. The yard needs some work, but you can do that yourself. This could be a really wonderful house, and I'm sure Gerald and I could help you. I bet Mark and Tyler would too. They helped me with mine, and they know everybody." Dieter sounded so excited. "I'd love to have you as my neighbor again. I missed you after you left."

Timothy stopped moving through the room and turned to Dieter. "I missed you too, but I couldn't stay here anymore." Timothy felt his knees threaten to buckle, and he forced himself to remain standing. He was not going to give in to the fear, not now, with Dieter here. He could do that when he was alone, but not now.

Dieter nodded before heading toward the stairs. "I still missed you."

Timothy forced his legs to move and followed Dieter to the second floor. It looked much like the first floor, except for a few rooms, one of which had been his. There were still some of the things he hadn't taken with him in there: some old pictures, the bed and dresser, the detritus of a life left behind. Timothy didn't look too hard; he really wasn't ready for that.

Leaving the room, they continued down the hall. The other two bedrooms were largely empty, but the fourth small bedroom looked as though it had been used as storage for everything his mother had no use for. "She could never throw a single thing away, the pig!" Timothy shut the door and added a dumpster to the list of things he was going to have to get.

"I bet if you pull up these old carpets…." Dieter knelt in one of the corners, pulling at the edge. "Look, there's oak under here. If you get rid of these, I bet the floors will be beautiful. You've got great woodwork, and mostly it just needs cleaning and touchups. This could be a really great house, and think how happy Grampy would be to see you here fixing the place up."

Timothy laughed, throwing his arms around Dieter's neck. "You just want the neighborhood eyesore cleaned up."

Dieter looked mortified for about two seconds before grinning. "Actually, I want my best friend back. It felt like you got ripped away when you left." Dieter returned his hug. "I know why you did it, and I don't blame you one bit, but it still hurt."

"I know, and I'm sorry," Timothy said, wishing more than anything that things had been different.

"Gerald will be home from work soon. Why don't you come back to the house? We can talk, and you can stay for dinner." Dieter grinned, and Timothy remembered what he'd been missing all this time. Growing up, Dieter had always acted like the big brother he'd never had, actually better than a big brother, because he was also his best friend.

"Are you sure Gerald won't mind?"

"Of course not," Dieter said, as they descended the stairs. They left the house, and Timothy locked the front door. Following Dieter across the yards, he watched as his friend bounded up his front stairs and held the door open for him. Inside, the house was a showplace, and Timothy stopped, almost in shock. He'd been expecting the house to look the same as it had when he and Dieter were kids, but it was so different, in a rather spectacular way. "Go on into the living room. I'll get something for us to eat and be right in." Dieter left, and Timothy wandered a little through the house, admiring everything.

"This is really nice," Timothy said as he stopped in front of the fireplace. The portrait above it looked familiar.

Timothy stared at the image. "Why does this look familiar?" Timothy had seen this somewhere, but he wasn't sure why.

"That's Gram when she was a girl," Dieter said from behind him. "Sometimes I find it hard to believe she was ever that young because I only knew her when she was old. It was hanging in the museum for a while. *The Woman in Blue* was Gram's mother. The portrait of Gram was part of the opening exhibit at the museum, along with the other works we were able to recover. I'm surprised you didn't hear about it.

The story was all over the news and stuff." Dieter looked hurt, and Timothy sighed.

"I've been really out of it for a while. Between school, working, and taking care of Grampy, I missed a whole chunk of what went on in the outside world." Timothy didn't know what to say. He hadn't meant to hurt anyone. "I'm glad you got the paintings back; they're really amazing," Timothy said, feeling uncomfortable and sort of figuring he should just leave.

Timothy turned to say goodbye, and Dieter's hand touched his shoulder. "I just missed you," Dieter said, and Timothy placed a hand on Dieter's. "It was like you ran away from me too." That was Dieter—sensitive as they came. He remembered the one time they'd fought as children: Dieter had looked as though his world was coming to an end.

"I didn't run away, Dieter, I got out," Timothy said softly as he tried to hold it together. After six years, the hurt was still close to the surface sometimes. "I worked after I graduated high school and went to college. It was a freaking miracle that I got this scholarship through the school so I didn't have to borrow all the money for my degree." He still had a mountain of debt, but he was working hard to pay it down.

"Where are you working now?"

Timothy smiled wide. "I got a job in the design department at Harley Davidson. I help design the motorcycles. I'm the junior associate in my department, but it's the coolest job ever." Timothy loved going into work every morning. The other guys who'd been there for a while thought Timothy a bit too enthusiastic, but this was his dream job. "I'm saving up to get a cycle, but I have bills to pay down, so that will have to wait for a little while."

"I'm glad you're doing well," Dieter said before bear-hugging him again. "I'm not letting you get away again. Even if you sell the house, I'll stalk you if you don't stay in touch."

Timothy laughed and returned Dieter's hug. It was good to have close human contact again. For a long time, he hadn't been touched like this, except for careful hugs with Grampy and Rose, but he had to be careful not to hurt either of them. Dieter, on the other hand, threw himself into the hug, and Timothy figured he must be feeling like his prodigal brother had returned, because that was a bit how Timothy was feeling right now. He hadn't even realized just how much he'd missed his friend until he saw him again.

"The house looks amazing," Timothy commented once Dieter released him from the hug.

"This house didn't look much better than yours when I got it. Gram did her best, but the house needed a lot of work. Initially, I did a lot of it myself, but Gerald has helped as well, and we've been able to make the house our own. Would you like to see the rest?" Dieter asked excitedly, taking Timothy on a tour of the entire place. It looked so very different from the way the house had looked when Dieter's grandmother had lived there. "I didn't want the house to look like a memorial to Gram, so we updated a lot of the rooms. Her bedroom was one of the last we did, but I had to bite the bullet and let it go."

"Do you think my house could look like this?" Timothy asked as he ran his hand over the fireplace mantel in Dieter's master bedroom.

"I don't see why not," Dieter answered. "These old houses have amazing character, and with a little care and some elbow grease, they shine right up." Timothy heard what he thought was the front door opening and closing. "That's Gerald," Dieter said, already heading for the stairs. Timothy followed more slowly, and when he reached the lower landing, he saw Dieter in the arms of another man, both of them obviously very happy to see each other. The wave of longing that came over Timothy nearly knocked him back onto the stairs. He wanted that kind of unabashed happiness more than he could say, and he hadn't even known it until that second. The realization made him understand why he felt so hollow inside sometimes. Timothy pulled himself together and headed the rest of the way down to where the other two men were standing. "Gerald, this is Timothy. He and I have been friends for years, and he owns the house two doors down. I'm trying to convince him to stay and fix it up." Dieter kept an arm around Gerald's waist as he made introductions.

Gerald extended his hand. "It's nice to meet you. Dieter has told me about some of the things you two did growing up."

"It's nice to meet you too, and I hope you won't hold those stories against me."

"Timothy is going to join us for dinner," Dieter explained, and Gerald nodded.

"I figured that part out," he said with a smile before turning to Timothy. "I was about to open a bottle of wine—would you like a glass?"

"That would be nice, thank you," Timothy answered, and he followed the couple back into the kitchen. It had obviously been recently remodeled, and every surface gleamed, from the granite countertops to the new cabinets that went beautifully with the rest of the house. His mind was already turning about what he wanted to do with his own house. Gerald opened a bottle of white wine and handed Timothy a glass before passing one to Dieter as well. He motioned toward a stool, and Timothy sat while Gerald and Dieter began pulling things out of the refrigerator.

"Is there anything I can do to help?" Timothy asked, feeling a bit useless watching them work.

Dieter returned to the refrigerator and began pulling out veggies. "You can make the salad, if you like." Dieter placed a bowl and cutting board near him, and Timothy began cutting vegetables.

"Do you remember the story Grampy always told about his mother during the Depression?" Dieter asked as he put a pot of water on the stove to boil and began shucking sweet corn.

"What was it?" Gerald prompted.

Timothy laughed at the memory. "Grampy said that his father had bought a brand-new car in early 1933. They must have had it for about a week when Grampy's dad was asked to travel from Philadelphia, where they were living, to Milwaukee. He went by train, and Grampy said that his mother became obsessed that someone was going to steal the car." Timothy took a sip of his wine when he finished cutting the lettuce, and then started on the tomatoes. "Grampy must have been about ten, and he told her to lock up the car. So his mother got a length of chain from the garage and padlocked the car to one of the trees planted by the curb. She stopped obsessing about the car and was happy until Grampy's dad got home and wanted to use the car." Timothy took another sip of wine.

"What happened?"

"It seems there was no key to the lock she'd used to secure the car to the tree." Timothy began to chuckle, saying, "And Grampy's dad spent an hour with a hacksaw, trying to cut through the chain so he could get his car loose."

"That's good," Gerald said with a chuckle.

"It gets better," Dieter added. "Because once he got the car free, he then asked his wife…." Dieter paused, and they answered together, "Why didn't you just park the car in the garage?" Both he and Dieter laughed, carrying Gerald along with them.

"Grampy used to tell me stories all the time," Timothy continued. "According to Grampy, it was when his dad was on that trip that he got the job offer to move to Milwaukee, and it was way too good to pass up. It was Grampy's parents who originally purchased the house just down the block."

"They must have had money, then," Gerald said, and Timothy nodded.

"They weren't rich, but even during the Depression, they lived pretty well. Grampy's dad was a talented executive, and he worked for one of the breweries in town after Prohibition, so he did very well," Timothy explained. "In fact, Grampy used to tell me about him and his dad visiting the Philadelphia Mint just before they left town. Grampy used to say that his dad knew that tough times were coming, so he drew a lot of his money out of the banks and converted it to gold in the late twenties. Before they left Philadelphia, they were supposed to turn in the gold coins for paper money, and Grampy's dad took him along when he did it."

"The government was nearly insolvent," Gerald explained, "so they made people trade in their gold for paper. It was good for the government, but it screwed a lot of individuals over later on, when times got tough again."

Timothy finished cutting the tomatoes and began working to clean the yellow peppers. "Grampy said that when they got to the mint, it was chaos. There was a huge line, and they had to wait a long time. He said a person in line was robbed, but the other people in the line caught the guy as he was trying to get away and nearly beat him to death.

"They waited in line for most of the afternoon in the blazing sun." Timothy tried to imagine how that must have been. Heavy clothes, loads of sweaty people, no shade or relief at all as everyone stood in line on the sidewalk. "The first thing they had to do was take the raw gold to the bullion window, where they got, of all things, gold coin for it. Then they had to take the coin to exchange it for cash. Grampy told me that by the time they got to the window, his dad was so fed up that he hid coins in his inner pockets and only turned in some of them. Grampy said that when they got to Milwaukee, his dad hid the coins somewhere in the house as a safeguard."

"Are they still there?" Dieter asked.

"I doubt it, after all these years," Timothy answered. "Grampy said there used to be a safe in the one corner of the basement, but it's gone now. You can still see the indentation in the concrete where it had once sat, and I suppose that's where anything would have been kept." Timothy finished up the salad as Dieter placed the corn in the boiling water.

"I'll light the grill," Gerald said, picking up the plate of steaks and heading toward the back door.

"Grampy used to tell me that story all the time." Timothy stood up and wandered to the island, leaning against the counter as Dieter finished cooking. "When I was a kid, I could almost hear the sound of the cars as they passed on the street and feel the sweat as well as the concern and panic that everyone had to be feeling at the time. Grampy told me everything seemed so uncertain, and everyone kept wondering what was going to happen next."

"I always loved listening to your Grampy's stories." Dieter stirred the corn in the huge pot. "What happened to him?"

Timothy sighed softly as he thought of his Grampy. "Mom put him into a home just before I left, and he did okay for a couple of years, but then he started to have circulation problems, and he lost his legs. He was better for a while then, but eventually the circulation problems spread to the rest of him, and his mind really started to go. He'd forget who I was sometimes, and toward the end, he didn't know anyone. He died a few weeks ago, and that's when I found out about the house." Timothy let the words taper off. The rest was still too painful to talk about. "It was a blessing, I know that, but I still miss him so much."

"I wish I'd have known," Dieter said softly, and Timothy nodded slowly.

"Mom put him in the cheapest place she could find. I tried to find a better place for him, but I couldn't afford it." Timothy swallowed as the guilt he'd mulled over so many times reared its head once again. "Towards the end, I used to just sit with him and hold his hand. I knew he didn't know me anymore, but every time I visited, I thought it might be the last time."

Dieter turned off the burner and set his large spoon aside. "Were you there when he died?"

Timothy shook his head quickly. "One night he went to sleep and didn't wake up. Thankfully, the home called me, because my mother didn't do anything for Grampy's funeral, including show up." Timothy could forgive a lot of things, but her treatment of Grampy…. Timothy could never forgive her for what she'd done to him.

"What was wrong with her?" Dieter asked. "She never looked very good when I saw her." He began removing the corn from the pot and set each ear on a plate.

"She was an addict." Timothy sighed. "My mother the crackwhore." At first, Timothy could see that Dieter thought he was kidding, but when Timothy nodded slowly, Dieter's mouth hung open. "She used drugs of some sort for a long time. Mostly pot when I was growing up, but about a year before I left, she started using harder stuff.

She tried to hide it at first, but after I figured it out and confronted her, she stopped hiding it altogether. I probably should have called the police, but she was my mom and I wanted to help her. As soon as I finished high school, I left."

"So that's why," Dieter said almost to himself.

"That's most of it, yeah. Like I said, she was mean to Grampy when he wouldn't give her money. She was mean to everyone. When she needed a fix, she would do anything." Timothy had found that out firsthand, but he couldn't bring himself to talk about that with anyone. "So I left."

"I always thought you left because you were treated badly," Dieter whispered.

"That's part of it too. Living on the street was better than living there, and by then she'd put Grampy in the home. Since I didn't have to look after him anymore, it was time to leave. I should have kept in touch, but Mom didn't know where I was, and I never wanted to see her again. So I cut all ties with everything here and stayed away." Timothy felt terrible that he'd run out on his friend, but at the time, he really hadn't seen how he'd had any other choice. "Can you forgive me?"

Dieter walked around the island, pulling Timothy into another hug. "I already have."

The back door opened, and Gerald came back into the kitchen, setting the platter on the table. Dieter brought over the corn, and Timothy carried the salad. Dieter got plates and utensils, and they all brought their wine glasses to the table. Gerald opened a bottle of red, and they all sat down. The three of them talked and laughed, dispelling Timothy's gloom. Gerald was a great guy, and he seemed to love Dieter deeply, which his friend really deserved. They talked about general topics, and when all the food had been devoured, they lingered at the table for a long time, drinking a little more wine and simply talking and laughing together. Timothy was careful about what he drank because he had to drive back to his apartment, and as the evening wore on, he got up to say good night.

Dieter walked him back to what was now his house, and Timothy decided to go directly home. "I'll be back tomorrow," Timothy told Dieter. "I'm going to start cleaning out the house and see what's there." Timothy wondered how he would feel being back in the house. Once he saw how he felt, he could decide what he wanted to do.

"It's Sunday, so both Gerald and I will be around. I forbid Gerald from working on Sundays because that's our time, so we're usually here doing projects and things around the house. So stop by when you get here, okay?" Dieter grinned, and Timothy walked toward his car with a much lighter heart than when he'd pulled into the parking space hours before.

Starting the engine, he waved and then pulled out, driving to his small apartment in Glendale. When he arrived, Timothy parked and went inside. Closing the door, he looked to see if anything was out of place. He always checked; it was an old habit. Everything was as he left it, but he did notice how sterile, almost clinical, it felt. He didn't have many things—he'd never needed them. But he'd felt a warmth at Dieter and Gerald's that he hadn't felt since he was a child with Grampy and Grammy.

Getting undressed, Timothy cleaned up and got into bed. Turning out the lights, he settled between the crisp sheets and tried to sleep. But it wasn't to be. Being back at the house had stirred up memories he thought he'd been able to bury.

THE next day, Timothy returned to the house and looked over at Dieter and Gerald's. Their place, like every other house on the block, was closed up tight at this hour of the morning. Since he hadn't been able to sleep, he'd decided he might as well get to work. On the way, he'd stopped at an all-night grocery and gotten trash bags. He'd also grabbed a bunch of cleaning supplies and had even stuffed the vacuum cleaner into the trunk. He had no idea what he was about to walk into, especially once he scratched the surface, and he wanted to be ready.

Opening the front door, he hauled in all the supplies and decided he might as well go room by room. He started in the easiest ones, throwing away the trash in the living and dining rooms before closing up his first trash bag and hauling it to the curb. He knew trash day was Monday, so he figured it wouldn't hurt for the bags to sit out overnight. Once that easy chore was done, he vacuumed the stained carpets in those rooms as well as the hall and then moved on to the kitchen.

That was a huge chore. Food had been left in the refrigerator, and he emptied it as quickly as he could, trying not to breathe, before shutting the door with a slam. He knew his mother had purposely unplugged it to make sure everything inside smelled as bad as possible. He'd brought some bleach, so he made a mild solution and wiped out the inside before giving up and closing the door for the last time. He'd just throw the whole thing away. Timothy cleaned out everything in the cupboards, making no decisions about whether it was good or not. Opening one of the drawers, Timothy gasped at the pile of needles and other bits of used drug crap he found. He dumped the entire drawer into the trash before moving on to the next. He spent hours in the kitchen and hauled bag after bag to the curb, but by the time he was done, the room smelled like Pine-Sol instead of musty death. Afterward, he looked at the basement door, but frankly he was afraid of what he might find and decided to put off that adventure for another day.

"Timothy," Gerald called as he made his way to the curb with the last of the trash from the main floor.

"Morning, Gerald," he called before dumping the bags on the growing pile.

"You've been busy," Gerald commented as he made his way over.

"I couldn't sleep, so I got an early start." Timothy looked at the pile of full, black trash bags. "I bought one of the huge boxes of bags, and that's only the main floor. I'm probably not going to have enough." Timothy smiled. At least he was going to have as much crap out of his house as possible. "I better get back at it if I ever want to get finished." Timothy headed back inside, waving to Gerald.

Timothy knew the upstairs was going to be worse, but he used the same strategy as downstairs. Most of the rooms didn't take too long, but the bathrooms were filthy and took a long time to clean and undisgustify. Timothy hauled load after load of bags to the curb, getting every room cleaned except for the one he knew was piled full. Standing in the hallway, he looked around and was deciding if it was time to get lunch when he heard a loud knock on the front door. Grabbing a load of trash, he descended the stairs and pulled open the door. He expected it to be Dieter or Gerald. He was not expecting to see his mother.

"What are you doing?" she demanded. "You can't throw away my stuff!" Timothy stepped back and tried to close the door, but she bustled inside the house. "All that is mine!" Her eyes looked glazed, and Timothy wondered what she was on now.

"I can throw away anything I like. I found all your drug crap, and I'll call the police and have you arrested right now if you don't leave. I bet they can find your prints on the syringes and other stuff. That, combined with the fact that you're high as a kite, should be enough to land you in jail."

"Is there a problem?" Gerald said from the doorway. "You need to leave. This house and everything in it are Timothy's to do with what he likes." Gerald sounded so confident that Timothy saw his mother waver, her head bobbing back and forth between them like some sort of demented bobblehead. "You are not to set foot on this property again."

"Or what?" she asked, folding her hands over her deflated-looking chest.

"You'll be arrested, and I bet if they do, they could find plenty on you." Gerald stared back at her, and Timothy stepped to the door.

"Get out now!" Timothy reached into his pocket and pulled out his cell. "All it takes is three buttons and your crackwhore ass is in jail!" Timothy was barely holding himself together.

"I'm still your mother," she said, stepping toward Timothy with her hand raised. Timothy braced for her attack but saw her stumble over the threshold, and she went flying, landing half in and half out of the door. When she got up, her nose was bleeding and her face was all scraped. She wavered and stumbled down the stairs.

"You stopped being my mother a long time ago, bitch!" Timothy cried before slamming the door. He looked out the window and saw his mother turn to look back, blood running down her face. She wiped it onto her blouse, barely noticing what it was. Timothy saw her get into a car, and after a few moments, it sped off. He didn't know if she was driving, but he heard Gerald on the phone.

"My name is Gerald Young, and I want to report a possible incidence of driving under the influence. I suspect both drugs and alcohol. A dark sedan, license number BRH-1208. The vehicle is probably heading west on Newberry toward Capital." Gerald explained Timothy's mother's behavior and provided additional information before disconnecting the call. "That should take care of them," Gerald said with a smile, shoving his phone into his pants pocket.

"Thank you," Timothy said.

"No problem. Dieter and I were about to get some lunch, and we were wondering if you'd like to go along. From the size of the pile of bags, you could use a break."

"I'd love one." Timothy didn't want to tell Gerald that he also really didn't want to be alone right now. "Let me wash up."

"We'll meet you at the house," Gerald said with a smile before leaving. Timothy locked the door and washed his hands in the kitchen sink before leaving the house. He met Dieter and Gerald at their place and rode with them to a small Middle Eastern restaurant. Once they were done, Timothy rode back and headed over to his house, with Dieter and Gerald right behind. They had insisted on helping, and together they tackled the room full of junk. There wasn't much in the room that was worth anything. Not that Timothy had thought there would be, but he had to look at everything before throwing it away. Finally, that room was done, and Timothy thanked Gerald and Dieter for their help. They had an appointment and had to go. "You call if your mother shows up again," Gerald told him at the front door.

"I will, and thank you both for the help," Timothy said at the front door before closing it behind them. He really wanted to go himself, but there was still more to do. He hadn't been in the attic yet, and he wanted to know if there was anything up there. His mother never went up there. When he was a child, he'd found out his mother had a fear of the attic and refused to climb the steps, so he'd often played amid all the stuff that Grampy and Grammy had put up there. After carrying out the last of the trash bags, he climbed to the attic door and opened it, slowly ascending the dark stairs.

When he reached the top, he located the light chain and pulled it. The light bulb came on, and dust motes floated in the air. Timothy saw that all the stuff was still there. Boxes and trunks lined the edges of the floor. The space wasn't full, but it never had been. He was simply amazed that Grampy and Grammy's old things were still there. Timothy walked around the room, which spanned the entire top of the house. Everything looked the same. Timothy bent down and opened the lid on one of the trunks filled with old clothes. He could hear Grampy's voice telling him how Grammy had once worn the dresses inside. Timothy picked one up carefully as he listened to Grampy's voice in his head telling him about the first time he's seen Grammy. He'd said it was love at first sight.

Setting the dress back in the trunk, he closed the lid and looked around some more. He smiled and moved one of the trunks aside. The small doorway was still there. When Timothy was young, he and Grampy had built a play place in the attic. No one knew it was there except the two of them. It was their special place. *Remember the stories, Timmy. I put it where you always played.* Grampy's voice played in his head. He had told Timothy that over and over again, and as Timothy stared at the door, he wondered if there could be something to Grampy's words.

He suddenly knew what Grampy had meant. *I saved it all for you, Timmy.* Whatever "all" meant. Kneeling on the floor, Timothy unlatched the door and opened it, peering inside. Of course he could see nothing, because he and Grampy had always used flashlights. But he didn't have one. Opening the door further, Timothy closed his eyes and remembered what the room looked like inside. He stuck his head inside again, and a small amount of light shone in through the open doorway, just enough that he could see the room was empty. Leaning further inside, Timothy ran his hand along the angled wall that formed the underside of the roof. Grampy had lined it for him before putting up the wall, and it felt smooth. Then his hand touched a ridge near the limit of his reach. He couldn't tell anything more, so he backed out of the doorway and stood back up. There was something there, or at least something was different.

Heart pounding, Timothy hurried down the stairs and out the front door, locking it behind him. He needed a flashlight if he was going to find out what was there. "It's probably nothing," he told himself more than once as he climbed into his car and sped off to the nearest drugstore. He told himself to calm down even as he entered the store and bought a cheap flashlight and some batteries. Then he hurried back to the house, his heart racing, and rushed back up to the attic, carrying the bag. Putting the batteries in the light, Timothy turned it on and climbed into the small door. There was definitely a spot in the ceiling where it looked like a hole had been cut and patched over. Pressing on the spot caused it to move slightly, and Timothy pressed harder, but it did nothing more than give a little. Backing out once again, Timothy looked around for something he could use as a pry bar and found Grampy's old toolbox. Inside, he found a handmade screwdriver and carried that back into the little hideout with him.

Wedging it into the edge, Timothy worked the piece of wood free until it fell onto the floor, but nothing followed. "This is stupid," he told himself even as he reached into the hole, feeling around the edge until his hand brushed against cloth. Timothy worked it free and pulled it out of the hole before backing out of the door for what he hoped was a final time.

The bag jingled as he carried it to the light, and it was heavy too. Opening it under the bulb, Timothy reached inside. Sure enough, they felt like coins, and with his heart racing, he grabbed a few and brought them into the light. They shone as bright and new as the day they were minted. Gold.

CHAPTER 2

GERALD stuck his head inside the doorway of Joiner's office. "I got a call from a friend, and it seems that he might need some legal advice. He'll be in the office at four thirty, and I thought you should sit in." Gerald was gone before Joiner could reply. Checking his watch, Joiner saw he still had some time and went back to the research he was doing. He'd joined the law firm of Prince, Graham, and Associates about six months earlier. Fresh out of law school, he hadn't realized just how much he had yet to learn. Gerald Young and Brian Watkins had been great to work with, probably because they made such a great team. Brian was one of the senior partners, while Gerald was a junior partner. Rumor had it that he was about to be made a senior partner, and Joiner could see why. He was driven and did amazing work. Joiner had read up on a lot of Gerald's and Brian's cases. They were brilliant attorneys, and Joiner loved that he got to work with both men.

"Have you got that research for the Garvin case?" Brian asked as he breezed into Joiner's tiny office.

Joiner sifted one of the files on the desk before handing Brian the one he needed. "I also e-mailed you the details," Joiner said.

"Thanks. I appreciate it," Brian said, breezing out of the office, and Joiner went back to his research. He had never imagined when he was in school the amount of research and mundane, dull tasks he would have to do in order to prove himself so he could get a chance at a real case. Not that he was complaining. He worked with great people, and they were showing him the ropes. Both Gerald and Brian often called him into client meetings to observe, like he would this afternoon.

A few minutes before his meeting, Joiner locked his computer and walked down the hall to Gerald's office. Gerald was waiting for him, and a man about Joiner's age sat in one of the chairs. Joiner entered the office, and Gerald motioned for him to close the door. "Joiner Carver, this is Timothy Besch," Gerald said, and they shook hands. "Joiner is a new associate, so he'll be sitting in to observe. Everything said in this office is subject to attorney/client privilege," Gerald said, and Joiner knew he was talking mainly to Timothy, but he was also reminding him as well.

Gerald looked to Timothy, who seemed nervous, and when Timothy stood up and looked at him, Joiner had to blink a few times. The man was adorable, with bright-blue, intense eyes and unruly hair that tumbled down his forehead. He looked a bit like a shaggy puppy, but even cuter, if that was possible. "Last week, I was cleaning out the house and something connected. This was the afternoon I had lunch with you and Dieter," Timothy said to Gerald, and Joiner listened to Timothy's voice the way he would listen to fine, complex music. "I found something that could be really important, but I'm scared to tell anybody, and I don't know what to do."

"Why don't you start at the beginning and take your time," Gerald prompted.

Timothy nodded nervously. "Grampy used to tell me lots of stories. And while he was at the home, Grampy kept telling me that he saved something for me and to look where I always played. When I was cleaning out the attic, I found the play area Grampy made for me when I was a kid. It was our place, and I realized that Grampy might have been telling me that he'd hidden something there."

"Did you find anything?" Gerald leaned forward in his chair as Timothy nodded. "Can I ask why you didn't come to me earlier?"

"Because I couldn't find Grampy's will right away." Timothy handed a set of folded papers to Gerald. "He left everything to me, but since he had nothing when he died, it really wasn't much good. I needed to make sure my mother couldn't show up and claim part of what I found."

"What did you find?" Gerald asked, and Timothy lifted the backpack he'd set beside his chair onto his lap and opened it, withdrawing a canvas bag that looked really old to Joiner. Timothy stood up and set the backpack aside before pouring the contents of the bag onto Gerald's desk.

Joiner had never seen so many gold coins in one place before. "My God," he said softly, but thankfully neither Gerald nor Timothy seemed to hear him.

"There were 149 coins in the bag, all five-, ten-, and twenty-dollar gold pieces. Here are 148 of them on your desk. Those coins aren't why I need your help." Timothy turned around and reached into his backpack once again, pulling out another coin that he'd placed in a plastic bag. "I already touched it, but I don't want anyone else to. I was looking up the value of these coins on the Internet, and when I got to this one, I found out plenty, and all of it's bad." Timothy set the bag on the desk.

"It's a Double Eagle twenty-dollar coin," Gerald said, picking up the bag. Gerald looked at the coin, and Joiner saw the color drain from his face.

"Exactly," Timothy said, and Gerald handed the coin to Joiner, who took the bag and looked it over.

"I don't understand." It looked like some of the others. Joiner thought the coin was gorgeous, but he didn't get what the problem was.

"Look at the date," Gerald explained, and Joiner turned the coin over.

"It's dated 1933," he said before looking back up.

"That is a 1933 Gold Double Eagle. Those coins were destroyed by the mint, and that coin," Gerald said, pointing to the coin in his hand, "is not supposed to exist. The federal government has been searching for and confiscating those coins for seventy years. In 1934, the government required all gold coins be turned in. The 1933 Double

Eagles had been minted but were never distributed, and all of them were destroyed, according to the government."

Timothy took the coin and placed it back in his backpack before gathering up the others, placing them all in the bag before putting it in his backpack as well. "I want you to find a way for me to keep the coin. It was Grampy's."

Gerald looked dubious. "We'll certainly try, but if I remember right, there were ten of these that surfaced the last time, and the Treasury Department confiscated them. They're supposedly in Fort Knox now. Let us do some research—we'll have to let you know what's possible." Timothy stood up and walked toward the door. "I suggest you get a deposit box to keep those coins safe."

"I will," Timothy said as he hoisted the backpack over his shoulder and left the office. Gerald looked concerned, and Joiner waited for him to speak. "I need you to research cases regarding any 1933 Double Eagles. There's at least two that I know of, because they hit the news, but there could be others. And while you're at it, research the Philadelphia Mint itself. There may be an angle there that we can use."

Joiner took notes as Gerald threw out ideas. "Is there anything else?"

"Yes. I'm going to ask you to take the initiative on this case for now. I know it's your first one, and I'll be with you the whole way, but I want you to think outside the box and see what you can come up with. I'm going to speak with Brian and Harold to fill them in, and you can get started. For now, treat it as a pro bono case, and I'll get Harold's okay." Gerald stood up to leave his office.

"Do you really think he'll go along with that?" Joiner asked. "I don't mean to question your judgment."

"We'll see," Gerald said. "Go get to work and see what you can find out."

Joiner headed for the door. "I will," he said excitedly and hurried out of Gerald's large office and back to his smaller one. He immediately unlocked his computer and began his research. He worked for a few hours and was so engrossed in it he didn't realize that Brian had stepped into his office.

"Joiner, go home," Brian said with a smile in his voice, and he looked up to see that most of the rest of the office was dark. "Whatever Gerald has you working on will wait until tomorrow."

"I'm just finishing up," Joiner answered as he bookmarked a page for tomorrow before shutting down. "I guess I lost track of time."

"That's a sign that you're doing something you love," Brian told him as they walked toward the elevators together. "Go out and have some fun. You work hard, Gerald and I both see that, but you're not going to make partner in the next three months." Brian winked at him. "It'll take at least a year."

Joiner returned Brian's smile as the elevator doors opened. They rode to the parking level together, and Joiner waved goodbye, getting into his small car while Brian climbed into his Mercedes.

Joiner knew Brian was right. He hadn't done anything fun in so long he could barely remember what it felt like to have fun, let alone sex or anything approximating it, with another person. Normally, Joiner got on the freeway and went directly home, but he decided to take Brian's advice to heart and headed across the river and into the bar district. Somehow he found a place to park, and after taking off his jacket and tie, he loosened his collar and got out of the car. He had no idea where to go. He hadn't been down to the gay bars in a few years, and while he remembered some of them, he really wasn't interested in the same atmosphere he'd wanted when he'd been in college. Thinking *what the hell*, he saw a sign for the Pink Triangle and walked to the front door, pulling it open.

Joiner had been expecting a smoky, dark gay bar. He had not been expecting a place with fresh air and huge video screens on the back wall. Guys were standing in front of the massive flat television screens playing video games with the others in the bar looking on, whooping and hollering as the scores climbed. "Can I help you?" the bartender asked as Joiner approached, still watching the screens.

"I'll have a beer," Joiner said absentmindedly.

"What kind?" He pointed to the board, and Joiner saw that they had twenty different kinds, most of which he'd never heard of. "We don't serve the normal stuff here."

"Why don't you recommend one that's not too heavy," Joiner said, and the bartender nodded and pulled a light-colored beer, setting it on the bar. Joiner paid him and took the glass, finding a stool farther down the bar. Guys were holding hands, and a few of them were kissing at the tables, but mostly everyone was watching the competition in the back. As Joiner looked around, one thing he noticed was that there didn't seem to be any of the usual "types" of guys. There were no guys leaning against the walls in "come look at me" poses. These looked like regular guys, geeks, even, and they were having the time of their lives. The room filled with the sound of jubilation as the game ended, with the winner patted on the back and handed a mug of beer. The players stepped back, and two more guys took their places as Joiner watched from the bar. Men moved all around, some watching, like Joiner, while others settled at tables to talk or do what gay men have done in bars for decades.

"Are you going to try?" a male voice asked from next to him.

Joiner shook his head before looking.

"It's you, from the law firm. I know Gerald introduced you, but I'm bad with names."

"I'm Joiner Carver," he said, extending his hand. "Gerald said your name was Timothy…," Joiner prompted.

"Yes. Timothy Besch," Timothy answered as the bartender brought him another beer. "You're going to be helping Gerald."

"Actually…." Joiner shifted on his stool so he could see Timothy better. Even in the dim, shifting light, the man was adorable, with the cutest button nose. "I'll be doing the initial research."

"Cool," Timothy answered, and a roar came up from the back as the game ended. "Do you want to take a turn?" Timothy stood up and motioned for Joiner to go. "It's a lot of fun." Joiner slipped off the stool, carrying his glass along with them. Timothy handed him a set of controls and explained what to do before picking up his own set, and the game began. Joiner quickly found he was completely hopeless, while Timothy was a natural, zooming around the racetrack dotted with mushrooms and waddling penguins with ease. Once the game was over, one of the other men wanted to challenge Timothy, so Joiner relinquished his controller and stepped away.

Timothy beat the man easily, and soon others were challenging him, but Timothy demurred and handed over his controller to someone else, and the games went on. "You didn't have to do that," Joiner said when Timothy joined him.

"I have the game at home, and I can play anytime," Timothy explained as he took a seat at Joiner's table. "Is this your first time here?"

Joiner nodded. "I haven't been out much lately, and I sort of happened in here by chance. It seems like a lot of fun."

"This has to be the only geek gay bar in existence. The owner made his money as a website designer. He opened the bar as an investment, and all his friends started coming here. The video games came next, along with the sci-fi movie nights, and gay geek heaven was born. I found this place my last year in college, and it's where I come when I want to be myself."

Joiner looked around the room. Some of the guys were overweight, others really skinny, and there were guys who wouldn't really fit in with the primped and polished crowd at some of the other bars. Yet Joiner felt comfortable here. There was no pretention, just fun, and, of course, boys being boys. "I think some of your friends are motioning you back to the game," Joiner explained.

Timothy looked back and shook his head. "I'd rather talk to you." Timothy smiled at him and bumped Joiner's shoulder, and he returned the smile. "It's been a long time for me," Timothy began, and then he looked down at his mug like he was thinking or mulling something over. "Do you like working at the law firm?" Timothy asked him.

Joiner had been expecting something else, but Timothy seemed to have changed his mind.

"It's great," Joiner said. "Gerald and Brian are really good to work with. Gerald said you were a friend."

"Sort of. I own the house a few doors down from them. His partner, Dieter, and I have known each other since we were kids." The sound of the video games died away and music began to play. "It must be ten o'clock."

Joiner looked around like he'd missed something. "How do you know?"

"Video games end at ten, and then the music starts. Do you dance?" Timothy asked, and Joiner shook his head.

"I look like some demented chicken when I dance," Joiner explained and picked up his mug, downing the last of the beer, thinking that maybe it was time for him to go home. But Timothy laughed and turned his head toward where some guys had gotten up.

"In a room full of geeks, do you think any of us move like Fred Astaire? Please, we're lucky if there aren't eyes poked out by the end of the night. Come on, let's have some fun." Timothy held out his hand, and Joiner figured what the hell, it wasn't every day that a cute guy asked him to dance. He figured he'd do his best not to hurt anyone.

The music changed as they walked out, and Timothy put his arms around Joiner's waist, holding him close as other guys did the same with their partners. It felt really nice to be held, and Joiner went with it. Resting his head on Timothy's shoulder, Joiner inhaled his scent and felt himself harden in his slacks. As Joiner tightened his hold on Timothy, he heard him sigh into his ear, and Joiner got the distinct impression that Timothy needed to be held like this just as much as Joiner did, maybe more. As they danced, Joiner could feel Timothy tense for a few seconds and then relax again. Placing his arms around Timothy's waist, Joiner slowly stroked up and down Timothy's back, feeling his muscles ripple and move beneath his shirt. Lifting his head, Joiner looked into Timothy's eyes and saw a longing and warmth he hadn't seen from anyone. Joiner was tempted to lean in and kiss

Timothy's lips to satisfy a growing curiosity about how the man would taste, but a gulf seemed to open up behind Timothy's eyes that Joiner couldn't understand as anything other than an old hurt reasserting itself. Not knowing what else to do, Joiner tightened his hold and continued slowly swaying back and forth. He kept expecting the music to change, but it didn't, and nothing happened to break the spell, so they danced and danced.

Eventually, the music did change, the cocoon woven around them instantly disappearing like a popped soap bubble. Timothy's arms slipped away, and Joiner stepped back, blinking as he looked around. The change jarred him, the loss of Timothy's warmth and touch a little unsettling, like something very right had just been ripped away for no apparent reason. Joiner had no idea why he felt that way or why he had an urge to ask someone, anyone, to change the music back. Joiner knew whatever spell had held them was over, and he could see that Timothy knew it too, by the way he was looking around the room like a scared rabbit looking for an escape route. Joiner backed away to give the other man some space. "Would you like something to drink?"

Timothy nodded once and then sank into a chair. Joiner walked to the bar and ordered two beers, paying for them before returning to the table. "I'm sorry, I usually don't act like that," Timothy said as Joiner approached the table.

"Like what?" Joiner asked as he set down the drinks. "We were just dancing."

Timothy picked up the glass and downed a quarter of it in a few gulps. "I was so forward." He actually looked a bit horrified. "I don't know what came over me."

Joiner chuckled softly into his glass. "You know, there's nothing wrong with asking for what you want." He could already feel the sexual energy inside him start to rise. Timothy was hot, there was no doubt about that, but as Joiner took another drink, watching Timothy over the top of his glass, he could see something vulnerable about him, like the rabbit analogy his mind had conjured up wasn't too far off. "And there's nothing wrong with being a little forward."

"Yes, there is." Timothy drank some more beer, and Joiner touched the glass, taking it from Timothy and lowering it to the table. "I always come here because I feel safe here. No one is going to hit on me or make any moves. I can be myself, and I don't have to worry. I guess I let my guard down, and I don't want you to think I'm some kind of tease or something."

Joiner smiled and touched Timothy's hand. "I don't think you're a tease. All we did was dance, and it was really nice. It's not as though we met for dinner and you ordered the lobster." Timothy looked at him blankly, and then a smile lifted the corners of his mouth. "It was a really nice dance, though. But I'm not expecting anything more, unless that's what you want." Timothy still looked a bit spooked. "Maybe I should go." Joiner finished his beer and stood up, walking toward the door.

"Joiner." He felt Timothy's hand on his shoulder. "I… I'm a little messed up, I guess." Timothy wouldn't look him in the eyes.

"Timothy, you don't owe me anything, and there's nothing to feel bad about." Joiner hadn't wanted to leave. What he really wanted was to spend a little more time with Timothy, but the man's discomfort was clearly evident. "I'll see you around, okay?"

"Could we maybe get dinner or something sometime?" Timothy asked, and Joiner almost said no just because of the completely mixed signals Timothy was sending. "I'm not very good at this kind of stuff; I never have been. That's why I come here, because it doesn't really matter. The guys are nice, and most of them are more interested in video games than anything else." Joiner followed Timothy's gaze and saw that a bunch of guys were playing again, but the volume couldn't be heard over the music.

"Hey, I think you did great, and I'd like to have dinner with you." Joiner pulled out his wallet and handed one of his business cards to Timothy. "Call me on the cell number—I'd be honored to have dinner with you anytime." Joiner smiled and left the bar, walking straight back to his car. Other than at work, Joiner really didn't expect to see

Timothy again. He'd definitely been attracted to him, and Timothy was most certainly cute, but the odds were that he'd never hear anything.

Joiner drove home and parked outside the back of his East Side apartment building. Inside, the place seemed quiet, and at first, he thought his roommate was out, but then he heard soft noises. Walking through the kitchen and back living room, which he used, Joiner listened at the doorway to the front room of the apartment and heard the definite sound of Marty and someone going at it. There was plenty of yelling, swearing, and God knew what else. Marty was most definitely bisexual, which in Marty's case meant he would fuck anything that moved. Returning to his portion of the apartment, Joiner flopped on the sofa and reached for the television remote. *So much for a night out.* He'd gone to a bar and had some laughs, got to dance with a really cute guy, and Marty was in his room reminding Joiner of exactly what he didn't have.

"God, Marty." A majorly pissed-off female voice rang through the apartment. "You are one sick pig!" He heard stomping and what could have been jumping as the pissed-off lady pulled on her clothes. A few minutes later, a small blur in pink sailed through the room.

"Come on, Cheri." Marty's voice preceded him, and when he appeared in the doorway, Joiner had to look twice. "It's sexy and playful." Joiner wanted to sink into the cushions, and he was seriously trying to figure out how he was going to be able to remove his eyes and brain to scrub them clean.

"No, it's sick!" Cheri said before flipping her blonde hair once and rushing out the back door.

"Dude," Joiner said, once she'd left. "I have to agree with her." Joiner allowed himself one last look.

"She said she liked babies," Marty explained with a shrug.

"Maybe," Joiner retorted. "But I doubt she meant that she wanted you to be one." Joiner managed to hold in the laughter at the sight of Marty wearing a white towel diaper and carrying a huge baby bottle for about two more seconds before bursting into near hysterics. He then reached for his phone and snapped a picture before Marty rushed at him. Joiner shoved the phone into his pocket before fending Marty off. "I'm not into babies," Joiner quipped as he reached for Marty's towel. "But I will snap your bare ass if you don't get away from me." He continued laughing as Marty left the room, his "diaper" almost dropping off his ass. "You're sick!" Joiner called, and Marty flipped him the bird before disappearing around the corner.

Joiner had seen Marty in everything from uniforms to bunny costumes, but this was the first time he'd seen him in a diaper, and he hoped it was the last time. "So I take it you went out after work?" Marty's voice drifted in from the other room, and a few seconds later, he wandered in wearing a robe, with no sign of diapers or other baby gear.

"Yeah. I ended up at the Pink Triangle. A new client and friend of Gerald's was there." Joiner wasn't sure what to make of Timothy, so he kept it light on the details. "We played some games and danced for a while, but then Timothy got nervous and started to back off."

"Maybe you were moving too fast," Marty said as he flopped on the sofa.

"That's just it—he was really nice when I got there, and I thought he was trying to put the moves on me, but then he backed off. He did ask me to dinner, though," Joiner added quickly. "I'm just not sure."

"You're asking me about guys?" Marty rolled his eyes. "Just because I've fucked a few doesn't mean I'm some sort of expert. You're the one into the perpetual sausage fest."

"Be serious," Joiner said.

"You like this guy?" Marty asked, and Joiner nodded. "Then see if he calls you for dinner." Marty's usual smart-aleck look faded away. "When people are in any bar, there's the expectation that they're there to hook up, especially a gay bar, and maybe this Timothy got worried that that was what you were thinking and he didn't want to be a dick tease. You said you danced together, right?"

"Actually, we slow-danced together for a long time." Joiner remembered how Timothy had felt and smelled in his arms, and the way Joiner had instantly reacted to him.

Marty nodded and spread his hands. "See—he probably thought he'd been leading you on. I know if I'd been slow dancing with a chick for a while, I'd expect that she was interested in riding my pogo stick."

"You think that about everyone," Joiner said with a smile. "Except me."

"You're different. You aren't interested in just hooking up, you never have been. You've been out with, what, three guys at most, and you dated all of them for months until they turned into complete losers."

"Gee, thanks."

"The important thing," Marty continued, talking over Joiner, "is that you aren't looking for a quick hookup. You want a relationship, and that's really cool. So don't sweat it over Timothy. If he knows what's good, he'll call you, and if he doesn't, it's his loss." Marty stood up and walked out of the room, returning a few seconds later. "By the way, dude, I have to go on a trip to install a printing press in Kuala Lumpur. I'll be gone for about a month, and you'll have the apartment to yourself, so raise the rafters at least once while I'm gone." Marty flashed a grin and Joiner rolled his eyes as Marty left the room. A few seconds later he heard Marty's bedroom door close. Joiner continued staring at the television until it was time to go to bed.

THE following morning, Joiner hurried into the office. He had plenty of work to get done for Gerald, and he really wanted to start working on Timothy's coin case. He was fascinated by the possibilities, but he couldn't get started on it until he finished up more urgent matters, so it wasn't until after lunch that he was really able to dig in. "Have you found anything?" Gerald asked, coming in and sitting in Joiner's single visitor chair.

"On the coin case? Not yet. I just got started," Joiner said, looking up from his computer. "Can I ask you something? Would it be unethical to see one of the firm's clients socially? I guess he's sort of my client, but he's more your client." Joiner squirmed in his chair.

"You like Timothy?" Gerald asked with raised eyebrows.

"You said I should go out, and when I did, I met Timothy at one of the bars downtown. He asked me to dinner, and I don't want to cause any problems if I go." Joiner had been thinking about that for most of the night.

Gerald began to laugh. "You going out with Timothy is fine. I think he liked you too. It seemed that once he got home, his first call was to Dieter, and they talked for quite a while. I won't go into details, but he was afraid he'd messed everything up." Shaking his head, Gerald stood up. "Let me know when you've got something, and I'm glad the interest in Timothy is mutual. From the little I know about him, he's already had a hard life." Gerald left the office, and Joiner got back to work.

He was just getting into the research when his cell phone rang. He almost let it go to voice mail when he didn't recognize the number, but answered it anyway. "This is Joiner."

"Hello, it's Timothy, from last night. I hope now isn't a bad time."

"Not at all, I'm glad you called." Joiner wondered just what had precipitated this particular phone call. He imagined Gerald calling Dieter, who called Timothy, who was now calling him.

"Umm, I was wondering if you would still like to go to dinner." Joiner heard Timothy take a quick breath. "You don't have to if you don't want to. I know we were drinking last night, and you were probably just being nice, so I'll just let you go now. I'm sorry for bothering you." Timothy's words tumbled out, and then the line went quiet, and Joiner figured he'd better answer or Timothy would hang up.

"I was hoping you'd call, and I'd love to go to dinner with you," Joiner said quickly, expecting to hear the line disconnect at any second.

"Really?" Timothy sounded like a little kid for a second.

Joiner chuckled softly. "Yes, really."

"I was afraid I'd probably scared you off with how I was acting last night. I guess I had a bit too much to drink and was acting a bit scattered. I'm kind of a lightweight." Timothy still sounded nervous, but there was energy in his voice as well. Joiner had picked up on that when they were playing games and even when they were dancing.

"What did you have in mind for dinner?" Joiner asked, figuring he'd get the conversation off the past and onto the future.

"Well." Timothy paused. "Gerald and Dieter are having a dinner thing tomorrow night, and I was wondering if you'd like to go with me. Dieter said there would be people there you'd know."

"I'd be happy to go," Joiner said, a little nervous that they were having dinner at his boss's. This could be very good or really bad. But Joiner had already agreed, and dinner with Timothy would be fun anywhere.

"Do you know where Gerald lives?" Joiner didn't, and Timothy gave him directions. "My house is two doors to the north. We can meet there at six thirty and walk to Gerald and Dieter's."

"I'll see you then," Joiner said, and he heard the call disconnect. Setting his phone on the side of his desk, Joiner stared at it for a few seconds, expecting it to ring and for Timothy to tell him he'd changed his mind, but it remained silent, and Joiner returned to his research for the rest of the day, making a lot of progress on Timothy's case.

At the end of the day, he knocked on Gerald's door. "Can I speak with you?"

Gerald looked up from his typing. "Ten minutes, and I'll call you," Gerald replied, and Joiner walked back to his tiny office. He made sure everything was together and ready, so when Gerald called, Joiner grabbed his files and hurried to his office. "What do you have?"

"A lot of material, and almost all of it is bad," Joiner said, and Gerald motioned him to the table. After closing the door, Gerald joined him, and Joiner opened his files, placing copies of the important materials in front of Gerald. "Thus far, thirteen 1933 Gold Double Eagles have been located. Timothy's would be the fourteenth." He didn't even think about using the client's first name even though he would never do that normally. "Two of them are in the Smithsonian, donated to them by the Treasury before the other coins were destroyed. One of them was auctioned off a number of years ago. That coin was purchased by King Farouk of Egypt, and according to the records I can find, which are limited because there was no actual litigation, the government agreed to the sale of the coin because they had actually issued an export visa for it in the forties, so it was semi-legitimate. At the auction, the winner had to pay the Treasury the twenty dollars in order to monetize the coin."

"What about the other ten coins?" Gerald asked. "I'm familiar with parts of that case, but not the details."

"The people who found them contacted the Treasury, which confiscated them. That case went to litigation, and the court did rule that the government had to prove that it had a right to seize the coins, though the court ultimately ruled in the government's favor because mint records indicated that none of the coins were placed in circulation and that none of the coins, other than the one auctioned, have ever been monetized." Joiner stopped talking and waited to see if Gerald had any questions before continuing. "The government's arguments centered around the faith and credit of the US monetary system. In essence, these coins were almost counterfeit because they hadn't been officially issued."

"That was a good presentation of the facts, but I also want your opinion. As a lawyer, one of the things we have to do is think outside the box. We can't try the same case they did, because we will lose. And in fact, it probably wouldn't even get to trial—the government would just immediately seize Timothy's coin." Gerald seemed so earnest, which Joiner had seen before. Gerald had passion for what he did, and that made him one of the best lawyers Joiner had ever met. "How much time have you spent on this?"

"Five hours," Joiner answered.

"Excellent. I want you to spend the remainder of the allocated hours trying to find an angle that we can use." Gerald sat back in his chair, thinking. "Look into the monetization process that the Treasury Department uses and see if you can find something that makes this case different from the others. We need something, or we're dead in the water."

Joiner stood up and gathered his files. "Also, on a personal note," Gerald said as he motioned toward the chair, and Joiner sat back down. "I understand you're coming to dinner tomorrow with Timothy."

"If you don't…," Joiner began, and Gerald raised his hand.

"I think it's great. Brian and Nicolai will be joining us as well, along with Brian's daughter, Zoe. It should be a casual evening with little shop talk. Please don't tell Timothy what you have or haven't found. He's bound to be nervous about it, but since he is a client, we need to make sure we separate our business and personal relationships. Once we have definitive answers, we'll call him into the office."

"Okay," Joiner answered and got back up, walking toward the door.

"One more thing. Let this go for tonight. Sleep and think on it, because we'll be taking on the United States Government with this case."

"I know." Joiner stepped out the door and then stuck his head back inside. "We do have one advantage. We already know the government's arguments, because they've used them before."

Gerald shifted his chair. "True, which means the court will expect us to have a rebuttal for each one of them handy. That's where our work lies. We have to rip apart the government's existing case." Joiner understood, and left Gerald's office, heading back to his. There was plenty of work ahead of him, because in the end, he wanted to see Timothy's smile when he told him the news.

*C*HAPTER *3*

TIMOTHY looked out the window one more time before walking to the bedroom he was using to finish getting dressed. For the past few weeks, Timothy had spent almost every spare moment working on the house, and there was still a lot to be done. But he'd pulled up all the carpets and had indeed found hardwood floors beneath. He'd cleaned them up for now, knowing eventually he'd have to have them sanded and refinished. He'd also painted many of the rooms on the first floor and had started on the upstairs bedrooms. The biggest job of all had been cleaning out the basement. Timothy had broken down and had a dumpster delivered, and he'd lost track of the number of trips he'd made up the old basement stairs, chucking away years of crap. At least now the house was empty, and cleaner than it had been since Grampy lived here. Opening the closet door, Timothy checked in the mirror to see that he looked okay before descending the stairs as the doorbell rang, or more accurately, fizzled softly. It was one of the things that needed to be fixed, and that list continued to grow, but Timothy was taking it one room and one project at a time.

He opened the door, motioning for Joiner to come inside, and Timothy's eyes widened when Joiner handed him a bouquet of bright-colored flowers. "Thank you," Timothy said, accepting them as he wondered if there was anything to put them in. "Let me put these in water, and I'll give you the tour of my construction site."

Joiner laughed, looking around. "Are you living here?" Joiner asked, and Timothy heard the touch of fear in his voice.

"No. I have a small apartment in Glendale. I'm fixing up the house, though I haven't decided if I'm going to sell it or keep it." Thankfully, Timothy found a jar in the kitchen and put the flowers in water. "There's still a lot of work to do," he explained as he led Joiner through the house. "This was my grandfather's house, and he left it to me."

"This is an amazing place," Joiner said as he twisted to look up the staircase banister. "Great character, and the floor plan works really well. Do you have a conservatory?"

"No," Timothy answered with a smile. He was pleased Joiner liked the house. "Mark and Tyler down the street do. Theirs is right off the dining room, and they keep it full of tropical plants. It's really nice, and it makes the house smell so fresh."

"So, you found the coins here?" Joiner asked as Timothy led him into the living room, their footsteps echoing in the empty room.

"In the attic, actually. I can show you sometime, if you want. Grampy used to tell me stories all the time, and one of them was the time his dad took him to the mint in Philadelphia when he was a kid. Grampy said he saved something for me and told me he hid it where I used to play." Timothy watched as Joiner wandered around the room, looking at everything. "He built me a play area in the attic when I was a kid, and it was still there. I found the coins hidden in that area, under the eaves." Timothy checked his watch. "We should probably go over to the party." He felt like he was running out of things to say.

"Of course," Joiner said, and Timothy led them to the door. "I was really pleased you called yesterday. I wasn't sure you would. You seemed a little nervous at the club."

Timothy opened the door and waited for Joiner before closing and locking it behind them. Then he stopped, standing on the steps. "I guess I wasn't expecting to meet someone I was interested in." Timothy held back a cringe. He hadn't meant to actually say something like that.

What if Joiner was just being polite and now he'd scared him away? "I know a lot of the guys there, and it's just a place that's comfortable." Timothy slowly descended the stairs and was a bit surprised when Joiner took his hand.

"So when you approached me, you were just being friendly?" Joiner supplied, and Timothy nodded. "Was dancing with me just being friendly too?"

Timothy stopped walking and shook his head. "I've danced at the club, but usually alone or with a group of the guys." Timothy allowed himself a smile that brightened when Joiner smiled too. "I haven't slow-danced with anyone in a long time." He tried to think of the last time and realized it had been years ago, when he was in college, and then he'd been dancing with a girl. "I wouldn't have asked you to dinner if I hadn't liked you." They stepped to the sidewalk and walked the short distance to Gerald and Dieter's.

"I like you too," Joiner said, and Timothy felt some of the tightness that had been building in his stomach for almost the entire day start to lessen. He liked Joiner, and he seemed like a nice guy, but Timothy realized he'd acted a bit loopy at the club. Thankfully, Joiner seemed to accept his rather lame excuse, because he was definitely not ready to discuss the real reason with anyone.

As they approached their destination, Joiner released his hand, and Timothy instantly missed the innocently intimate touch. Ringing the bell, he waited, and Gerald opened the door a few minutes later. Please come in," he said brightly, ushering them inside. Dieter was right behind him, and Timothy was instantly pulled into a hug.

"Dieter, this is Joiner Carver."

Dieter shook Joiner's hand. "Gerald has told me a lot about you," Dieter said in his usual excited tone. "Everyone is in the living room," Dieter added as he motioned before leading the way, and Timothy felt Joiner's light touch on his lower back. It felt nice and a bit protective, which was nearly a foreign concept to him. With the exception of Grampy, no one had protected him except himself for a long time.

When they entered the living room, Gerald made introductions. "This is Timothy, our neighbor, and Joiner, a newly minted attorney," Gerald began before going around the room. "Mark and Tyler, Brian and Nicolai, their daughter Zoe, Sean and Sam, their son Bobby, and his partner Kenny." Greetings and handshakes were exchanged. They took the empty chairs, and Dieter brought drinks. There were snacks on the table, and they helped themselves.

"What do you do, Nicolai?" Timothy asked the man sitting next to him, but he didn't acknowledge the question.

"Nick can't hear you," Zoe said as she tapped Nicolai's shoulder and began signing to him.

"I'm an art restorer," Nicolai said rather haltingly.

"Cool. Have you worked on anything famous?" Timothy asked.

"Nick worked on all the art for Uncle Dieter and Uncle Gerald, including *The Woman in Blue*. He also does regular maintenance for the Chagall windows at the Art Institute in Chicago." Zoe was obviously proud of her father's partner.

"Zoe, Nick can speak for himself," Brian chastised very lightly, and Timothy saw Nicolai smile at the young lady, signing to her. The two of them had a silent conversation for a while, and then Nicolai pulled Zoe into a light hug and released her. "Parties are difficult for Nicolai," Brian explained. "He has difficulty knowing where to look. He's not being rude if he appears to ignore you. He tries to read lips, but sometimes gets overwhelmed."

To Timothy's surprise, Joiner began signing, and he watched him. "You're very good," Zoe said, "but you got 'peace' wrong," and she proceeded to correct him.

"Zoe, that's rude," Brian said.

Joiner said, "No, it's not. My signing is probably a little rusty. I had a childhood friend who was deaf, and I learned to sign some time ago, but haven't used it much recently." He signed something to Zoe, and she giggled and then looked to her dad with one of those "see, I was right" looks.

Dieter announced that dinner was ready, and everyone filed into the dining room, where a huge table was set. Timothy and Joiner took their places near the end of the table, with Kenny and Bobby across from them. Dieter and Gerald brought bowls and a platter of steaks to the table, and everyone began to talk as the food was passed around.

"What do you do?" Joiner asked Kenny as he passed Timothy the platter of meat.

"I'm on the Milwaukee police force," Kenny answered rather seriously. Timothy saw Bobby nudge him in the ribs, and Kenny's posture seemed to loosen up. "Sorry. I get used to being really serious at work."

"Kenny's a big teddy bear," Bobby teased. "He's up for detective this year." It was obvious that Bobby was very proud of his partner. "I'm an artist," Bobby volunteered.

"Joiner works with Gerald and Brian, and I'm a design engineer for Harley. How long have you been together?" Timothy nibbled on his steak while waiting for pasta and veggies.

Bobby looked wistfully at Kenny. "I guess about six years, officially, but we've been friends since we were teenagers," Bobby said with a still-in-love smile. "Kenny's dad was Sam's partner on the force for years, and when he died in the line of duty, Kenny came to live with us. I realized I was in love with him when we went off to college, but we didn't become a couple until we graduated."

"Sounds like quite a story," Joiner said, and Timothy felt him squeeze his hand under the table.

"You know," Bobby said, waving his fork slightly, "but around this table, there are plenty of stories. I was living on the streets before Dad rescued me and gave me a home."

"Really?" Timothy asked, and Bobby nodded before leaning across the table.

"I have a story too," Zoe said from the other side of Timothy. "I helped catch some men who broke into our house last year. They were trying to steal Nick's stained-glass window, and I got to visit the FBI and everything." Zoe looked proud of herself, and Timothy looked at Brian, who nodded his confirmation.

"Nick restored a Tiffany window, and the burglars were trying to steal it. Zoe saw them, and her keen eyesight and memory helped the FBI and Interpol catch the thieves. It turned out they'd stolen the Tiffanys from the Milwaukee Conservatory of Music as well."

"I read about that in the paper," Joiner said before leaning closer to Zoe. "That was you?" He put up his hand and the two of them high-fived.

"How did you meet?" Kenny asked across the table.

Timothy felt his cheeks color slightly. "This is sort of our first date. We met at Joiner's office and then at the Pink Triangle downtown a few days ago." Joiner lightly bumped his shoulder, and Timothy smiled and bumped Joiner back.

The conversation continued around the table through the rest of dinner. Joiner talked a bit with Gerald and Brian. Timothy noticed that they did not talk about work, which was a bit of a relief as well as frustrating. He wanted to ask if they'd found out anything, but before Joiner had arrived, he'd reminded himself that this was fun, not business.

Dieter and Gerald cleared away the dishes, and when Dieter returned, he was carrying a tray with individual cups of what looked like chocolate and whipped cream with a touch of fruit. "Chocolate mousse," Dieter announced, and Timothy noticed a few couples looking at each other sheepishly. "I know a dirty mind is a terrible thing to waste, but not around my dining room table." Most of the others began to laugh. Timothy looked at Joiner and shrugged, figuring it was one of those inside jokes people develop over time. Once dessert was served, Dieter brought coffee and sat back down at the table.

"So what exciting case are you working on now, Gerald?" Tyler asked from the far side of the table.

Gerald laughed. "Don't get many cases as exciting as going after *The Woman in Blue*." Timothy saw Gerald reach for Dieter's hand. "Or as rewarding." Gerald looked at Dieter, his eyes filled with love. Timothy almost brought up his case, but he felt Joiner nudge his leg, like he could read his mind, so Timothy turned his attention to his dessert instead. After dinner, everyone returned to the living room for an evening of conversation.

Brian, Nicolai, and Zoe were the first to leave, and shortly afterward the party really began to break up. Timothy and Joiner said their good-nights, and Gerald followed them to the door. "We should have something for you later this week. Joiner will call you to set up an appointment at the office." Gerald smiled at him, and Timothy wasn't sure if he should be excited or scared. He'd read the news reports of the other coins that had turned up, and he knew bad news meant that the coin would be taken away. Timothy searched for some sort of answer in Gerald's face, but there was nothing to be found. "Timothy, we don't know yet, but we will." Gerald touched his shoulder, and Timothy nodded, deciding to trust his old friend's partner.

"I'll see you at the office tomorrow," Joiner said to Gerald as he shook his hand.

"Oh no you won't," Dieter said lightly. "It's Saturday, and Gerald had promised me an entire weekend that I fully intend to collect on. You'll see him early Monday." Dieter looked about as excited as Timothy had ever seen him, and that was saying something.

"The boss has spoken," Gerald said with a happy nod. "I'll see you on Monday, and I suggest you have some fun this weekend too."

Joiner turned to Timothy with a look Timothy couldn't quite understand. "I'll do my best." Gerald and Dieter closed the door, and Timothy wondered just what Joiner had meant as they walked back toward his house. "Does Gerald usually give good advice?" Joiner asked, and Timothy knew from his tone that it was a leading question.

"As far as I know," Timothy answered, and he felt Joiner take his hand.

"Then I think we should follow it. I know it's short notice, but I was wondering what you had planned for tomorrow?" They had stopped walking, and Timothy looked deeply into Joiner's eyes, trying to discern his motive, but all he saw was sincerity and openness.

"I was going to try to get another bedroom painted and then tackle cleaning out the attic," Timothy answered, wondering what Joiner had in mind.

"I wield a mean paint brush. I could help with the bedroom, and then maybe take you to dinner and a movie," Joiner offered.

"You don't have to help me paint, but I like the dinner and movie part." Timothy stepped toward his front stairs.

"Then I'll see you tomorrow," Joiner said before leaning close, giving Timothy a light kiss. "Good night." Joiner turned and walked toward his car, waving before getting inside. Timothy watched as he drove away and then unlocked the house and went inside. He could still feel the touch of Joiner's lips as he got his things together and left the house before driving to his apartment. Timothy could hardly believe he'd just been kissed, or how much he liked it. And later as he got into bed, it was all he could think about. Well, that and the fact that he was seeing Joiner again.

THE following morning, Timothy arrived at the house after going to the paint store, and carried the supplies into the house and up the stairs. After turning on the radio, Timothy spread the drop cloths on the floor and opened the paint. He stirred it, then picked up his brush to begin painting, but he heard a knock on the front door. After putting down his brush, Timothy walked through the house and opened the door to see Joiner smiling back at him, wearing paint-spattered clothes, carrying a bag and a drink holder with what looked like two large cups of coffee.

"I told you I wield a mean paint brush," Joiner said as he stepped inside.

"You didn't have to do this," Timothy said, taking the bag as Joiner handed it to him. "But it's very sweet of you." The smell of hot cinnamon rolls drifted out of the bag, and Timothy's stomach growled. "I really don't have anything here to eat on."

"We'll make do," Joiner explained, and they went into the kitchen, standing at the counter. Joiner pulled out the rolls and tore open the bag to eat on, and they devoured the sticky, gooey, heavenly rolls standing up, licking their fingers the entire time. Once they were done, Timothy rolled up the trash and placed it in one of the bags. "Just a second," Joiner said. "You have something on your face."

"Where?"

"Here." Joiner held him and kissed him. Like the night before, the kiss was soft and gentle, but unlike last night's kiss, this time Timothy could feel the heat just below the surface. Timothy wanted more, and he returned the kiss, tasting the cinnamon and sugar on Joiner's lips until the kiss softened again and their lips parted.

"It's been a long time since anyone had kissed you, hasn't it?" Joiner asked, and Timothy nodded. "Why?"

Timothy forced himself not to squirm out of Joiner's arms. "It's a story I really don't want to talk about." He sighed and looked away from Joiner's deep eyes. He really thought he'd put all that behind him, but now he was realizing that all he'd done was bury it.

"Okay. I won't push you, but I'll listen when you're ready." Joiner released him slowly, and Timothy stepped back, trying to clear his head from the strange mixture of desire and fear that seemed to be gripping him. Every time Joiner kissed him, Timothy's mind turned to complete mush, but then the fear kicked in, irrational and nearly overpowering. He knew he needed to talk about this, but he wasn't sure he could. He'd hidden it all away for so long he didn't know how to do anything else.

"Thank you," Timothy muttered, swallowing hard before moving farther away from Joiner's embrace. He didn't know what to say, or where to look, for that matter.

Joiner seemed to sense his discomfort. "Why don't we get to work?" Timothy breathed a sigh of relief that Joiner was letting the issue drop and led the way upstairs into the bedroom to be painted. "This is a great room," Joiner said, as they stepped into the bright bedroom. "Was this yours?"

"Yes." Timothy had boxed up everything portable and carried it to the attic. The old furniture had nearly fallen apart when he'd tried to move it, so he'd thrown most of it away. There had been very little of importance left in the room, mostly things he wanted to forget. "When Mom and I moved in with Grampy, this was my room. Grampy used to sit on the edge of my bed and tell me stories before I went to sleep. We didn't have a lot, but Grampy made the most of whatever there was."

"What about your mother?" Joiner asked, and Timothy shook his head.

"I think about her as little as possible," Timothy said flatly. "Do you like to edge or roll?" he asked immediately, hoping Joiner would understand that he didn't want to talk about her.

"I'll edge," Joiner said, taking the brush, and Timothy could see the confusion and concern in Joiner's eyes. Timothy got the roller pan set up, letting Joiner edge a section of the room before beginning to apply the paint to the walls in slow, even runs of the roller.

"What's your family like?" Timothy asked to break the silence and tension that seemed to have settled in the room.

"I have an older brother and sister. My folks divorced when I was a teenager, and both of them have remarried." Joiner dipped his brush in the paint, wiping off the excess before continuing. "Mom and Dad talk, and they seem to have become friends after the divorce. My stepmother is okay, but Mom's second husband is amazing. He loves her to death."

"I bet it was hard splitting your time between families," Timothy said as he refilled the roller.

"Sometimes, especially right after Mom remarried. Carter, her second husband, tried really hard with the three of us kids, but we weren't ready to accept him. And I know it hurt when my sister Susan refused to attend the wedding. But Carter is Carter, and he remained kind and understanding, no matter what we did. He wore us down or grew on us, I'm not sure which." Joiner smiled, and Timothy did as well. "He's good to all of us. My father is a schoolteacher, and he does the best he can for all of us, I know that."

"But you don't get along?" Timothy asked, and Joiner shook his head, setting his brush down.

"Dad has a tough time with the gay thing. He does his best, and I have to give him credit, but it's hard for him. I also know he sometimes feels second-best. Carter has money—he paid for me to go to college and law school. Not all of it, I had to pay part, but Carter made it possible for me to attend Harvard, which I could never have done otherwise. He did the same sort of thing for Susan and Chet."

Timothy swallowed hard. "You went to Harvard?"

Joiner chuckled. "Yeah," he said in a Boston accent that made Timothy giggle. "I paaked at Haavaad Yaad. In Boston the R practically disappears sometimes." Joiner went back to edging the wall. "Where did you go to school?"

"Here in town. I needed to stay close and help take care of Grampy. I did it all myself, though I'll be paying for college for years, but I did it." Timothy was very proud that he put himself through school. He considered it one of the major accomplishments of his life. "And I'm a really good design engineer."

Joiner chuckled. "I bet you are." Timothy looked to where Joiner stood on the ladder and saw him wink at him. Thankfully, the conversation moved to other, lighter topics, and they worked happily for a few hours, getting the first coat of paint on the walls. Timothy had done the ceilings earlier, so they hadn't had to worry about those.

Timothy wrapped the brush and roller in plastic wrap and set them on the plastic drop cloths. "Ready for lunch?" Joiner asked.

"Yes. We'll need to give this coat a few hours to dry and then we can finish up with a second coat. You can use the bathroom down the hall to wash up," Timothy explained before heading to the downstairs bathroom. A few minutes later, he heard Joiner on the stairs.

"Timothy!" Joiner yelled through the house. "There's someone passed out in your front yard." Timothy turned off the water and hurried to the front door. Joiner had already opened it and was rushing outside. Timothy followed and stopped at his front stoop. He instantly recognized his mother. Her face carried the bruises from her earlier fall at the house, but that appeared to be the least of her injuries. One of her arms rested at an odd angle, and she was moaning softly. Joiner was already kneeling next to her.

"Joiner, don't!" he called as he saw him touch her. He wasn't sure why he felt so strongly that he didn't want Joiner touching her, like she'd contaminate him somehow.

"Timothy, she needs our help," Joiner said, but Timothy shook his head. He knew she was beyond anyone's help, but still…. Timothy pulled out his phone and dialed 911, telling them what they'd found, asking that both an ambulance and the police be sent. Closing the phone, Timothy stayed where he was and waited for help to arrive. He could not bring himself to come any closer to her. This was his own mother, but she was worse than a stranger.

Sirens sounded in the distance, breaking him out of his thoughts. Hurrying down the walk, Timothy flagged them down and then got out of the way as they rushed across the lawn, asking questions he couldn't answer. Joiner backed away as they approached, and the EMTs got to work as police cars began to arrive.

"Did she say anything?" one of the EMTs asked. Timothy said nothing, and Joiner shook his head. "Do either of you know what she's on?" Joiner shook his head, and Timothy wanted to do the same.

"Crack, probably," Timothy answered, letting his eyes lose focus so he wouldn't have to see the looks of anyone around him, especially Joiner. He was aware of how his reaction would look to others, especially once they found out who she was, but Timothy could not get involved with her in any way.

The officers spoke with the EMTs before walking to where Joiner and Timothy stood. "Do either of you know what happened?"

"No," Joiner answered. "We were working inside the house and about to get some lunch when I saw her on the lawn." He looked at Timothy, who shrugged and kept quiet.

"You told the EMTs that she might have been on crack. How did you know that?" The officer asked Timothy as he held open his notebook.

Timothy did not want to answer the question, but he couldn't lie. "Biologically, that woman is my mother." He heard Joiner gasp softly. "But in reality, she's the devil incarnate." Timothy turned away and went inside the house, closing the door behind him. He managed to take a few steps before his legs threatened to give out, and he leaned against the wall, letting it hold him up. This was too much, and he slid down the wall. He'd spent years staying away from her, avoiding her, trying to make sure she stayed out of his life completely.

The door opened, and Timothy looked up as Joiner hurried inside. Then he was being held tightly. Timothy clung to Joiner, not knowing what else to do.

"It's okay. I don't know what happened, but it's going to be okay," Joiner soothed.

Someone else came in, and Timothy expected it to be the police officer, but it was Dieter. Timothy was hugged again, this time by both of them.

Someone else joined them. Dieter and Joiner stood up and helped Timothy to his feet. "The ambulance is taking her to the hospital. Is there anything you can tell us?"

"The last time she was here, there was some boyfriend or someone waiting for her in the car." Timothy's mind refused to work very well. "She was high at the time. We called the police and reported the license number of the car they were driving." Timothy looked to Dieter. "Gerald made the call." That was all Timothy could remember as the pain of what she'd done to him came rushing back full force. He couldn't hold it in any longer, but he couldn't talk about it, either, so he knew he had to deal with it somehow. "Thank you for coming," Timothy told the police officer as he left the house.

"Are you okay?" Joiner asked, and Timothy looked at both of them.

"What do I have to do to make her stay away forever?" Timothy asked. He knew his voice was shaky. "I just want her to go away and leave me alone." Timothy took a deep breath, trying to will himself not to cry. He'd shed way too many tears over her, and he wasn't about to do it again. She wasn't worth it, because Lord knew she had never shed a tear or given a thought to the pain she'd caused him.

Dieter walked to the front door and peered out one of the small side windows. "It looks like they're getting ready to go."

Timothy nodded and slowly walked to the bathroom. He closed the door and refused to look in the mirror. Splashing cool water on his face, he tried to push out of his mind the way his mother had looked crumpled on the lawn, rebuilding the walls so he could keep the flood of conflicting feelings in check.

A soft knock sounded. "Are you okay?" Dieter said through the door.

Timothy wiped his face on a paper towel and opened the door. "Yes." He felt much more in control of himself now. "Go on and spend the day with that fantastic husband of yours, I'll be just fine." Timothy hugged Dieter, and he could tell Dieter was reluctant to leave, but Timothy shooed him out the door. Then Timothy looked around for Joiner and found him sitting in the single chair in the kitchen.

"What did she do to you?" Joiner asked in a whisper as he stood up.

Timothy shook his head violently. "I can't talk about it. Not now." He really expected Joiner to press him, but instead he was hugged tight, and he sighed against Joiner's chest, closing his eyes and trying to let go of some of the fear.

"As I said, I'll listen when you're ready." Joiner settled his hand on the back of Timothy's head. "Are you ready to get some lunch?"

Timothy nodded, and they left the house. Joiner drove to a small family restaurant, and they ate in relative quiet. Timothy really didn't feel like talking, and Joiner didn't press it. Timothy had been afraid he'd feel uncomfortable just sitting quietly, but it didn't feel weird or strained, just quiet and companionable, which was exactly what he needed.

CHAPTER 4

JOINER sat quietly through lunch, watching every move Timothy made. He was more than curious about what had happened between Timothy and his mother. At first, Joiner had been scandalized at Timothy's attitude toward his own mother. That had been shocking, but he had come to realize that there was more than Timothy simply not liking his mother and acting vindictive. Something was definitely wrong in that relationship, and if Timothy's mother was using, as Timothy had indicated to the police, that could explain the reaction. But something in Joiner's gut told him that was only the surface, and that something much more insidious had happened. If his mother were only using, then Timothy would probably want to get her help. Joiner's guess was that she'd hurt him very badly at some point.

He was very curious about Timothy's story, but he knew he couldn't push, so at lunch he simply kept him company. In the afternoon, they returned to the house and put a second coat of paint on the bedroom walls. "Would you like to take a walk?" Joiner asked once they were finished cleaning up. "I have clothes in the car I can change into."

Timothy thought for a second. "That would be really nice. The smell of paint is beginning to get to me."

"Let me get my clothes, and I'll be changed and ready in about ten minutes." Joiner hurried to his car and retrieved a small duffel bag. Back inside, he used the downstairs bathroom to change. By the time he was done, Timothy had put on fresh clothes as well and was waiting for him in the entry.

"Where do you want to go?" Timothy asked as he locked the front door behind them.

"How about the park? It's just a few blocks," Joiner suggested. Timothy seemed agreeable, and they walked north before crossing over to Lake Drive.

"I'm sorry for being so flaky," Timothy said after being quiet for a long time.

"We've all got things in our past that we don't want the world to know. Just because yours made an appearance today doesn't mean you're flaky. Like I said, when you're ready to talk, I'll listen." Joiner took Timothy's hand, and they walked quietly, just holding hands almost the entire way to the park.

As they entered the park, Timothy stopped. "I've been dying to ask if you found out anything on my coin."

"Right now we've just started doing the research. I really don't have an answer for you. I've found out a lot, but you want to know if it's good or bad, and I can't tell you that," Joiner answered as truthfully as he could. They walked into the park, heading down the paths toward the bluff that overlooked the lake. "Right now, all we have is information, and it's really hard to know what you have until the entire picture is together."

"You should know if you're finding good stuff or not," Timothy said, and Joiner shook his head.

"You never know. I worked on a case that looked really bad until we got all the information, and then we won the case easily. Sometimes a legal case can hinge on one fact or one piece of evidence. Gerald said you would probably ask, and he told me that I had to finish my work." Joiner turned to look at Timothy. "I promise we'll do the best we can, but it's too soon to give you a good answer." *And too soon for me to tell you that it doesn't look very good.*

"So does it look bad?" Timothy asked, and Joiner laughed, tapping Timothy on the butt before taking off across the lawn. He'd hoped Timothy would chase him, and he didn't disappoint. In fact, Timothy was fast, and Joiner had to dodge a few times to keep from getting caught.

"You're persistent," Joiner called as Timothy made another attempt to catch him. "But I can't tell you anything more." With another laugh, he let Timothy catch him, and they both toppled onto the grass, Timothy laughing, deep and rich. It was the first time Joiner had heard him actually laugh, and he wanted to make sure Timothy did it more often. His face came alive, and little crinkles formed around his eyes to meet his smile. Without thinking, Joiner turned to Timothy and kissed him, not long, but deeply. He'd have kissed longer, but he remembered they were in the middle of the park, and even in this part of town, they didn't need to be asking for it. Getting up, Joiner helped Timothy to his feet and took his hand once again, leading them deeper into the park.

The late-afternoon sun poked through the trees as they crossed the ravine bridge, heading into the next section of the park. They passed statuary and crossed walking paths as they ambled through the lush green woods and lawn. "I love it here," Timothy said as they walked through one of the heavily wooded areas. "It's like having a forest in the middle of the city."

"That's what these parks were meant to be," Joiner explained. "When they were built, people had small lawns, so this was meant to be the place where they came to play or just spend time. The park was meant to act like their backyard." Joiner began leading them back to Timothy's. It was getting late, and they needed to think about dinner.

Once they got back to the house, Timothy checked the windows in the room with the drying paint, and then Joiner drove them to a small bistro he knew. He wanted a place that would be small and not too busy. He got the small part correct, but they were swamped, so he and Timothy sat down to wait for a table. Timothy sat quietly while they waited, and Joiner touched his hand to let him know he was there.

Joiner had no idea what else he could do, and he was beginning to think his attempts to distract Timothy weren't actually helping at all.

"Have you ever had something really bad happen to you?" Timothy asked so softly Joiner barely heard him.

Joiner thought a few seconds. "I don't think I've ever done anything really bad, and I can't remember anyone doing really bad things to me." Joiner began wondering where Timothy was heading. "I think the most traumatic thing in my life was my parents' divorce. I've done stupid things, like the time I nearly set my sister's hair on fire. But...." Joiner shook his head slowly. "No, something really bad hasn't happened to me. I guess the bad things that happened to me only appeared bad at the time. If it wasn't for Mom and Dad's divorce, Mom wouldn't have met and married Carter, and he's always been good to all of us. Why? I know something happened to you, and I suspect it involves your mother."

Timothy nodded and looked out the window. "I don't think my mother ever loved me."

Joiner felt like he'd been punched in the gut. The idea was unfathomable to him. Joiner was loved by both his mother and his stepmother. He knew that. The admission shouldn't have come as much of a surprise, given Timothy's reaction to his beaten mother lying on his front lawn, but the idea was so foreign to Joiner that he could hardly get his mind around it. "I'm sure that's not true," Joiner said, because it seemed like what he should say, but the look in Timothy's eyes when he turned to look at him told Joiner otherwise. Timothy truly believed his mother didn't and had never loved him.

"Gentlemen, your table is ready," the hostess said. Joiner was about to ask if Timothy wanted to leave, but he was already on his feet, following the hostess to their table. Following behind, Joiner sat down across from Timothy.

"We don't have to stay if you don't want," Joiner said, faced with Timothy's dour expression.

"I'm sorry. I didn't mean to ruin your dinner," Timothy said, and he blinked a few times. Joiner knew he was trying to lighten his own mood. "I'm a terrible date, and when you asked me to dinner yesterday, I was so looking forward to this." The part about his mother ruining it wasn't said, but Joiner could read it in the touch of anger in Timothy's eyes.

"I've been looking forward to it too," Joiner said before deciding to try to change the subject. "Have you decided if you're going to keep the house? I think you'd told me you were still trying to figure out what you wanted to do."

"I haven't decided yet, but I'm leaning toward keeping it. There are some really good memories there, especially with Grampy, and I know he'd be happy that I'm fixing it up." Timothy took a deep breath, held it, and then let it out. "At first I was afraid of how I'd feel being in the house again, but the more I work on it, the less weird it feels." There was a touch of excitement in Timothy's voice. Joiner felt relieved and picked up his menu. Their server came and took their drink orders.

"So after the painting, what project is next?" Joiner asked.

"I have a painter who's going to paint the outside, but I need to get all the shrubs cut back before he comes. I'll probably just pull them out and replant. I also need to do something with the kitchen. The bathrooms are serviceable, but the kitchen really needs some help. So I thought I would see about having the counters replaced and getting some new appliances, maybe some fresh paint, and eventually I'll remodel it completely, once I can get the money together."

"You sound excited," Joiner said, as Timothy began to smile slightly. Just like at the park, his face lit up. "You know, you have a great smile," Joiner added quickly.

"I do?" Timothy asked, looking very surprised.

"Yeah, your eyes light up and you get this little dimple on your cheek." Joiner leaned forward so he could whisper. "It's really cute and very sexy." Timothy blushed deep red but didn't look away. "You should definitely smile more often."

Timothy shook his head. "No, I'm not. I've never been cute."

"Yes, you are," Joiner said. "Do you think I kiss just anyone? I thought you were off the adorable scale when I saw you in Gerald's office, and then at the club, you only added to it. You're a good person and very attractive, but not just on the outside. Like today, you got help for your mother even though you were obviously hurting. No matter how you were feeling, your innate goodness shone through."

"It's been really hard." Timothy looked at the table. "When I was a senior...." Joiner nearly groaned when their server brought their drinks because it looked to him as though Timothy was at least contemplating opening up to him, but now he could almost see the door closing again. The server took their food orders and left the table.

"You were saying...," Joiner prompted, but Timothy shook his head.

"It was nothing." Timothy took a gulp from his beer, and Joiner waited silently, hoping Timothy would change his mind.

"I don't think so," Joiner said. Going for broke, he reached across the table and touched Timothy's hand. He could feel Timothy's tension jolting right through him. "What are you afraid of?"

Timothy looked up, and the sadness and fear in his eyes made Joiner want to shake someone. "That if I tell you the story, you'll run away and never look back," Timothy answered, and Joiner could see it was the truth.

"That will not happen," Joiner said emphatically, and Timothy scoffed lightly.

"It has before," Timothy said blankly. Their server brought their meals, and Joiner tried to keep a smile on his face and his attitude positive even as his stomach turned and the food he tried to eat tasted like nothing. It had been a long time since Joiner had had such a nerve-racking and anxious dinner. Timothy was nervous, because he'd in essence agreed to tell Joiner what happened, and Joiner was worried about what had happened to the other man—overall not a recipe for a pleasant evening meal.

Once they were done, Timothy insisted on paying, as a thank-you for Joiner helping in the house. Together they walked to Joiner's car, and he drove to his apartment. "My roommate is out, so we have the place to ourselves," Joiner explained. Once inside, Joiner got a bottle of wine and poured them each a glass before sitting on the sofa next to Timothy. He said nothing, because everything that ran through his head sounded like a cliché or just plain lame, so he held Timothy's hand and sipped from his glass.

Timothy took a gulp of his wine and then another before setting the nearly empty glass on the table. Joiner could feel Timothy's hand shaking in his.

"I think it was early spring and Mom had just put Grampy in the home. I hated her for doing that and spent as much time as I could with my friends. After eating dinner with Dieter, I walked home, and as soon as I walked inside, I knew something was very wrong. Mom was in the hallway, and she couldn't stand up, and all I could hear was her begging for some sort of fix or other. This strange man I had never seen before was standing over her asking for money that she didn't have." Timothy drained the rest of his glass, and Joiner saw him shaking like a leaf. Joiner reached out to hold him, but Timothy moved away.

"Up till then, she'd been pretty good about hiding what she was doing, and I honestly didn't know how bad off she was, but I saw the man look at me for a split second, and then he grabbed me by the arm and yanked me over to my mother, saying he'd hurt me if she didn't pay." Timothy took a deep breath and continued shaking.

"What did she do? Did he hurt you?" Joiner asked, unable to take it anymore. Joiner embraced Timothy in a tight hug as he felt anger rising from deep inside.

"He kept threatening for a while, and Mom continued begging him for a fix. For as long as I live, I will hear how pathetic she sounded." Timothy was on the verge of tears, but he held it together.

"What happened?" Joiner asked, and he felt Timothy stiffen in his arms.

"You know that an addict will do absolutely anything to get a fix? Well, my own mother told this guy that if he'd give her the drugs she wanted, he could have me."

Joiner could not stop himself from gasping in horror.

"He yanked me into the living room and threw me onto the sofa. Before I knew what was happening, my pants were around my ankles, and he was... he was... he raped me." Timothy gasped for air, and Joiner slowly rubbed his back, trying to soothe him so he could breathe. "It hurt like hell, and I remember screaming and screaming as he ripped into me. The more I screamed, the more he seemed to like it." Tears ran down Timothy's cheeks. "When he got off me, he laughed as he pulled up his clothes, and I tried to climb under the sofa cushions. I could still hear my mother begging, and the next thing I knew, I heard my mother rushing to the bathroom. Then the front door closed, and I lay there for a long time, afraid to move and afraid he was going to come back. Eventually, I only heard Mom in the house, and I went upstairs and cleaned myself up as best I could. I was bleeding bad and didn't know what to do, but it slowed and stopped. All I could think of to do was disappear, so I grabbed a blanket and a pillow and snuck up into the attic. I spent the night hiding in the room Grampy made for me, and once I heard Mom leave for one of her intermittent jobs, I grabbed my stuff and left. I managed to arrange to start college in the summer instead of the fall, so other than a single return trip to get some more of my stuff, I never returned home again. Thank God I was eighteen and had a job. Before I left, I was hiding my money from her because Mom would take it, so I had something to live on for a little while until I could move into the dorms." Timothy seemed drained, and Joiner held him, rocking slowly back and forth. "My own mother let some guy rape me so she could get drugs."

Joiner seethed and realized if he'd have known this earlier in the day, he would have let Timothy's mother rot before helping her. "None of that was your fault," Joiner said as softly and soothingly as possible. "Did you tell anyone?"

Timothy shook his head. "I stayed away from her and tried to forget it. The next time I spoke to my mother was when I evicted her and her boyfriend, or pimp, or whatever he is, from the house. I don't even think she remembers what she did. But I have no doubt she'd do something like that again if she needed a fix bad enough."

"You never told anyone but me?" Joiner's head reeled at the level of trust Timothy had bestowed on him.

"I told a guy in college that I liked, and I thought he was interested in me. His name was Dale, and I really liked him, maybe loved him. We'd gone out a few times, and he seemed so nice to me. He'd asked about taking our relationship further, and I thought I could trust him. I told him some of what happened. I never finished, because he looked at me like I was dirt under his shoes, which is how I've felt for such a long time. He actually called me a liar and said that if I'd really been raped, I would have gone to the police. Then he said I probably liked it and couldn't deal with it. I never saw him again, and I haven't told anyone else, ever."

Joiner wanted to kill all three of them, Timothy's mother, the guy who'd hurt him, and the asshole from college. He thought all three of them should be taken out and whipped. Joiner was so angry and upset he began to shake, and Timothy pulled away, but Joiner held him tighter.

"I'm not mad at you," he said softly into Timothy's dark hair. "I want to kill all three of the people who hurt you." Joiner stroked his hand through Timothy's hair. "What happened was not your fault at all, and if I get my hands on any of them…." Joiner swallowed his words because he felt Timothy stiffen in his arms. "Dale was a complete ass not to believe you."

"You believe me?" Timothy asked as he tilted his gaze to Joiner's.

"Of course I believe you." Joiner leaned forward and lightly kissed Timothy on the lips. Joiner sensed that Timothy had done enough talking, so he sat back on the sofa and just held him quietly in his arms. They must have sat together for hours, and eventually Joiner heard Timothy's breathing even out, and he realized Timothy had fallen asleep. Joiner didn't want to disturb him, so he continued holding Timothy until he began to nod off, as well. The slight movement from Joiner jolted Timothy awake.

"I should go home," Timothy said sleepily as he sat up.

Joiner stood up and extended his hand to Timothy, who looked at it and then him a little dubiously. "You trusted me with your secret, so please trust me with this too," Joiner said, and he led a quiet Timothy back to his bedroom. "I'll be right back."

Joiner went into the bathroom and quickly cleaned up, setting out a fresh toothbrush and other things he thought Timothy might need. Returning to the bedroom, he saw Timothy sitting on the edge of the bed, looking a tad lost. "I put out some things for you."

Timothy got up and walked rather blankly to the bathroom. While he was gone, Joiner undressed to his underwear and got in bed, leaving the light on for Timothy.

Timothy saw him in bed, and Joiner patted the mattress next to him. "You're not...."

"No, Timothy. Just slip off your pants and shirt. All I'm going to do is hold you. I promise," Joiner said and watched as Timothy slowly pulled off his shirt, turning around before toeing off his shoes and slipping his pants down his legs. Timothy was pale, but lean. Narrow hips and a small butt complemented what he saw from the back, and when Timothy turned around, Joiner's mouth went dry. Timothy wasn't muscular, but he had faint lines on his belly and a slight chest. Joiner wanted to reach out and touch, but he figured Timothy wasn't ready for that, so he waited for Timothy to come to him.

Pushing back the covers as an invitation, Joiner made sure that Timothy saw he was wearing his underwear as well, and that seemed to allay some of his fears.

"Are you sure? I could just sleep on the sofa," Timothy said.

Joiner got out of bed, walking toward Timothy the way he'd approach a skittish animal. "You can sleep on the sofa if you want, but I'd rather you slept with me." Joiner placed his hands on Timothy's shoulders, lightly stroking his warm, smooth skin. "I will never do anything to you that you don't want. I can promise you that. There's no need to be nervous or scared." Joiner lightly kissed Timothy's shoulder and then backed away. Timothy had to make up his own mind, and Joiner was not going to force him. Getting back into bed, Joiner watched as Timothy stepped closer and then lifted the covers, carefully joining him on the bed.

At first Joiner didn't move, and he still left the light on. Then he rolled over and wrapped an arm around Timothy's waist, stroking his skin slowly. "You're really handsome, Timothy." Joiner stayed still, just holding and lightly stroking until he felt Timothy move closer. Then Joiner held him tighter before reaching to the night table to turn off the light. "Just relax. All we're going to do is sleep." Joiner yawned and rolled onto his side, tugging Timothy closer. When Timothy rolled over, Joiner spooned to his back, inhaling the intoxicating scent of this beautifully fragile man.

"I'm sorry I'm such a baby," Timothy said just above a whisper.

"Hey. You shared a secret with me, so I'll share one with you. Before that day when I met you at the Pink Triangle, I'd never played video games before."

Timothy rolled over in Joiner's arms before lifting his pillow and whapping him over the head. "That's not a secret. Every guy in the club could tell you were a greenhorn. You fell off a cliff eight times in the first game, and that lasted only four minutes. I swear you spent more time getting back on the track than you did actually riding on it."

"I know," Joiner said. "I can't see in the dark, but I bet you're smiling right now." Joiner reached out and lightly stroked Timothy's cheek. He just wished he could see it.

Holding Timothy close, he hugged him and waited for him to settle.

"Joiner," Timothy mumbled quizzically.

"It happens," Joiner said with a chuckle. "I can't help it when I'm around you. It'll go away pretty soon." There was no way he could keep from getting excited with Timothy right next to him, his skin under his hands, Timothy's scent surrounding him. Joiner heard a soft sigh and then Timothy settled on the mattress, rolling over once again, and Joiner spooned to him and closed his eyes. He wasn't sure how much sleep he was going to get, but a sleepless night was worth having Timothy next to him.

HE DID indeed spend a sleepless night, but it was the best one he could ever remember. A lot of the time, he simply lay next to Timothy, listening to him breathe. A few times, he wondered if Timothy was doing the same thing to him, but when he checked, Timothy actually seemed to have fallen asleep. The one thing that surprised Joiner was the sheer level of attraction he felt for Timothy. He'd been with other people, and he'd had a number of boyfriends, but none of them made him feel the way Timothy did. He was sure it wasn't just protectiveness, although he didn't doubt that was part of it, but he knew in the morning Timothy would need to go home, and he knew he'd miss him as soon as Timothy got out of the car.

In the morning, they slept late, and once they dressed, after spending a great deal of time kissing and grinning at each other like idiots, Joiner took Timothy for a nice breakfast before dropping him back off at his house. As he predicted, by the time he got back to his apartment, Joiner had the urge to pick up his phone to call Timothy, just to hear his voice. Joiner spent most of the day trying to get chores done he hadn't had time to do during the week, and in the evening he fell into bed and was instantly asleep.

Monday was a hugely busy day, as they always were, and it wasn't until late in the day that he finished the research for Timothy's case and went to see if Gerald was still in the office. It looked as though he was packing up to leave as Joiner knocked on his door. "I think I've done what I can with Timothy's case," Joiner explained. "When you have some time, can we go over it?"

Gerald hesitated, but then motioned toward the table. "No time like the present," he said as he set down his bag and pulled out a chair for himself.

Joiner handed Gerald a copy of the file he'd built. "The first page highlights what I found. I was able to discover a few other coins that have come to light. There wasn't much on them because one was from the forties and another in the fifties. All of them were confiscated by the Treasury on the grounds that they were property of the US Government." Joiner pointed to the second point. "Even the one that was eventually sold was at first seized, but the Treasury and the owner came to an agreement, probably because an export visa was issued by the government, so it was quasi-legitimate, and the Treasury probably figured they had a good chance of losing in court on that one."

"So you're giving up?" Gerald asked, and Joiner shook his head.

"You asked me to think out of the box, and I came up with a possibility. But it's a bit of a long shot. I think the only way anyone could keep one of the coins would be to prove that it had been monetized somehow. If it were, the government's hands would be tied, because once the government monetizes the coin, it transfers it to someone else and gives up ownership. Until then, the coin or bill is government property. I don't know how you prove monetization, though." Joiner flipped his file and passed the papers to Gerald. "The case of the ten coins hinged on the fact that they didn't know the origin of the coins. Does Timothy?"

Joiner saw Gerald's eyes widen. "I believe he does." Gerald reached to his bag and pulled out a legal pad. "His grandfather told him a lot of stories, and as I recall, one of them explains where the coin came from. I think we need to meet with him for an update, and let him decide how he wants to proceed. He could decide to keep the coin secret until government policy changes, and if he does, we lock up the records and forget about all of it. That doesn't sound like Timothy, but it's his choice."

Joiner began gathering up the papers, putting them back in the files. "When do you want him to come in?"

"Tomorrow afternoon, if he can," Gerald said, and he gathered his things, placing his copy of the file in his bag, "Very good job." Gerald headed toward the lobby while Joiner walked back to his desk. Picking up the phone, Joiner dialed Timothy's number. "Hey, how are you doing?"

"Good," Timothy said with a smile in his voice. "Actually better now that I'm talking to you. What's up?"

"I met with Gerald, and he asked if you could come in tomorrow afternoon. There are things we need to discuss and some decisions you need to make." Joiner tried to keep his voice as professional as possible.

"What time should I be there?" Timothy now sounded nervous, and the initial happiness had slipped out of his voice.

"Is four o'clock okay?" Joiner asked, and when Timothy agreed, he went on. "I'm about to leave the office and was going to stop and get some dinner. Would you like to join me?"

Timothy hesitated before agreeing.

"You don't have to if you're busy," Joiner explained.

"I'm just nervous, that's all," Timothy explained, "and dinner would be great."

"Where should I pick you up?"

"I'm working at the house."

"I'll be there as soon as I can," Joiner said, and after packing up, he hurried out of the office, saying good night to those working late. Once in the parking lot, he got in his car and tried not to break too many speed limits in his anticipatory excitement.

THE following afternoon, Joiner kept expecting a call from reception telling him that Timothy had arrived. He was obviously running late, and Joiner had informed Gerald that he would call to let him know when Timothy had arrived. He was about to call Timothy's cell when his phone rang, and Joiner jumped before snatching up the receiver. The receptionist informed him that Timothy had arrived, and Joiner stopped by Gerald's office on his way out.

"Bring him in here," Gerald said, and Joiner nodded before walking to reception and then escorting Timothy to Gerald's office.

"Please sit down," Gerald said to both of them. "Would you like coffee or a soda?"

"No, thank you," Timothy said, looking quite nervous.

"Okay," Gerald began, and Joiner could tell he was all business. "We've done a lot of research and we have"—Joiner heard him hesitate—"problematic news for you. The 1933 Double Eagle coins, according to the government, were never issued, and it is true that the Secret Service has investigated and seized any that have come to light. Only one was ever allowed to circulate, and it was sold a few years ago at auction." Timothy look crestfallen, and Gerald continued. "Don't give up yet. We do have some things working in our favor. In the last case, the government won, but the court did make the government prove they had a right to seize the coins. That could work to our advantage. Also, the people who had the coins did not know how they were originally acquired. I believe you know how your grandfather got his coin."

Timothy nodded vigorously. "I told you and Dieter the story at dinner a few weeks ago."

Gerald smiled, and Timothy clicked his pen in anticipation. "The thing is, we need as much detail as your grandfather told you. Please be careful to only include what he told you, rather than your impressions. This story and any of the details it holds could help us."

"I don't understand how," Timothy said.

Both Joiner and Gerald chuckled slightly. "We don't either, Timothy," Joiner explained as he looked at Gerald for confirmation, receiving it in the form of a nod. "But we need to know anything you can tell us. It could be important." Timothy didn't look convinced. "Your grandfather told you those stories for a definite reason."

Timothy nodded and began to tell the story of Grampy accompanying his father to the mint. "Grampy said it was really hot, with no place for them to get out of the sun as they waited in line."

"What time of year was it?" Joiner asked as he paused from his writing.

"Grampy said it was April and an unusually hot day. Everyone was still dressed in heavier clothes, which made it worse. Grampy said he was so uncomfortable because his mother had dressed him in wool that itched something terrible." Timothy smiled, and Joiner continued writing down every detail. "They had to go to the bullion window first, because Grampy said his dad had acquired some small gold bars and he didn't want to travel with them. I think the reason Grampy remembered this story was because his dad had told him that a law had been passed that required them to turn in their gold coins and when they took the bars to the gold window, they got more gold coins that they were supposed to turn in for paper money. It seemed really dumb to Grampy."

"Is that where you think he got the 1933 coin?"

Timothy nodded. "Grampy said his dad remarked on it when they got home, wondering why the government had made the coins and then turned around and passed the law that they had to be turned in," Timothy explained. "I used to ask Grampy all kinds of questions whenever he told this story because it sounded like the government was just dumb, especially to a young kid." Timothy grinned. "Now I know better, and like everyone else I'm *sure* the government is dumb."

"Why didn't he turn in all the coins?"

"Grampy told me his dad didn't trust banks or the government, so he refused to turn in all his coins and hid some of them instead. Gold was gold, and they'd already had three tough, fear-filled years. I think the amazing part is that the coins came down through Grampy's dad to Grampy, and then to me. I wish I knew how that happened. Because I bet there's a really good story there." Timothy alternately looked to Joiner and then Gerald. "So what do we do?"

"What do you want to do? All the other coins are yours, and you can do what you want with them. As far as the 1933 one goes, you can keep it and tell no one, if you want. The government won't know, and no one will come after you," Gerald explained, and Joiner watched Timothy's reaction and saw him shake his head.

"I want the coin to be mine," Timothy said. "What do we have to do? I'll pay you whatever it takes." There was a lot more bravado in Timothy's voice than in his eyes. They spent a few minutes going over potential costs.

"The first step is to contact the Secret Service. They'll investigate and should be able to authenticate the coin."

"Won't they try to seize it like they did with the others?" Timothy asked. "Because once they take it, it'll take years for me to get it back. I read what they did to those people who found ten of them in Philadelphia." Joiner could see the concern in Timothy's eyes. To most people, these were just coins, but Joiner was really beginning to see that to Timothy they were part of a legacy from his grandfather, and therefore so much more than just bits of gold.

"Leave that to us," Gerald said confidently, leaning back in his chair.

CHAPTER 5

GERALD had assured him of what he wanted to do, and while Timothy had his doubts, he trusted Gerald, and he'd agreed to the initial course of action. Now, two days later, he received a call from Gerald to come to his office. Timothy was nervous, but he trusted both Gerald and Joiner. Getting out of the elevator, Timothy walked to the receptionist, patting his pocket to make sure his tiny package was still there.

"Go right on back, they're waiting for you in Gerald's office," the receptionist told him, and Timothy pulled open the door and walked through. Joiner approached him, and Timothy smiled nervously.

"There's nothing to worry about," Joiner told him as he escorted him into Gerald's office where two men in suits were standing, obviously waiting for him.

"Timothy, these are Agents Gilliam and Forrester with the US Secret Service. They would like to see your coin," Gerald said, and one of the men stepped forward, reaching into his pocket, pulling out a badge.

"Please turn over the coin as property of the United States Government or face arrest," the man Gerald had identified as Gilliam said, in what sounded like some stereotype of a bad television show.

Timothy looked at Gerald and Joiner for direction, and he saw Gerald slowly get up from behind his desk. "That's not going to happen. I knew you would try this, and Mr. Besch has come down here in good faith. I also need to tell you that you will not be leaving with anything you didn't walk in here with. If you like, you are welcome to look at the coin, but that is all. If you wish to stake a claim, then you must do so in the courts. Because, you see, you made a mistake. You don't even know if the coin is genuine. If it isn't, you don't have a claim, and to determine that you have to see it." Timothy marveled at the way Gerald kept his voice level and calm, even as his own stomach turned over and over. Joiner stood next to him and lightly touched his hand, bolstering his courage. "Do we have an agreement? If not, you can leave now and try to get a court order for what might be authentic or one of those cheap reproductions sold on late-night TV. It's your call." Gerald motioned toward the door.

Timothy glanced at Joiner, who looked like he was trying not to smile as they waited out the agents. "Agreed, but if it is genuine," Agent Forrester explained, "we will not hesitate to get a court order for the coin's return."

"You can try," Gerald said with a half smile, and Timothy saw doubt pass over the agents' eyes just for a second. "Just to make it clear, we're agreed," Gerald said. They obviously didn't like it, but both agents agreed, and Gerald picked up his phone and called out to the lobby. A few minutes later, two large men stood at Gerald's door. "Just so you don't get any ideas," Gerald said before turning to Timothy. "You can show them the coin now."

Timothy pulled the coin, now in a plastic container he'd purchased at a coin store, out of his pocket. Gilliam reached for it, and Timothy pulled the case back. "He can look at it, but not you." Timothy did not like Gilliam at all, and Agent Forrester stepped closer and took the case, examining both sides of the coin. He then withdrew a loupe from his pocket, and after placing the coin on the table, he bent down to take a better look while saying nothing. Timothy kept his eyes glued to the coin the entire time. When he was done, Agent Forrester stood back up and stepped away from the table.

"Thank you, gentlemen, we'll be in touch." Agent Forrester walked toward the door, with Agent Gilliam right behind him.

"Joiner, I need you to get over to the federal courthouse. If my hunch is right, they'll head right over there, and we need to be there when they show up." Gerald picked up the coin and handed it to Timothy. "You shouldn't be carrying this around any longer."

"I won't. I'll put it back in the deposit box as soon as I leave," Timothy promised as Gerald left the office with him.

"I need to get over to the courthouse. I'll drop you at the bank on the way." Gerald grabbed his case, and Timothy followed behind him as he strode through the office. In Gerald's black Mercedes, they pulled out of his parking space and rushed out of the lot. The bank Timothy used was right around the corner, and it didn't take him long to put the coin back into the deposit box. Gerald was hanging up the phone as Timothy got in the car.

"We need to get to the courthouse now. If those agents get a court order, we'll be bound to comply with it." Gerald stepped on the gas, and five minutes later he was parking in the lot at the courthouse. Timothy was struggling to keep up with him as he hurried into the building. They went through metal detectors, and Joiner hurried up to them.

"They made a beeline for the second floor just a minute ago," Joiner explained, and Gerald strode to the elevator. They rode together, and when the doors opened, Timothy saw the two men talking to someone before entering a room. Gerald walked right up to the door, pulling it open and following them inside.

"What is that?"

"One of the courtrooms," Joiner said. "Come on. Sit in the back and say nothing." Joiner pulled open the door, and they sat on a bench at the back of the room.

"Court is not in session," the judge was saying as he walked to where Gerald and the two agents, along with another man, waited for the judge to approach.

"We understand, Your Honor," the man Timothy didn't know explained. "We have an order we'd like you to review and sign."

The judge took the paper and turned to Gerald. "Why are you here?"

"I'm the attorney for the person whose property they are trying to seize without due process," Gerald explained, and Timothy could see the surprise on the judge's face as he appeared to read the order.

"Can you prove this is the property of the United States Government?" the judge asked the agents.

"I examined the coin myself, and it appears genuine. Since none of those coins were ever issued by the government, the coin remains the property of the United States," Agent Forrester explained, and the judge looked to Gerald.

"The courts have already ruled in other cases of these specific coins that the government must prove it has the right to the property in question."

"I believe they proved that in those cases," the judge explained. "Unless there's something further, I'm inclined to sign the order." Timothy's heart sank, and he turned to Joiner, closing his eyes. This was exactly what he was afraid of.

"In those cases, they did prove it with those coins, but not this one, and the government must prove its right to seize property from each individual on that case's merit. The coin in question has been in the possession of my client and his family since 1933. And furthermore, in the previous cases, the holders of the property did not know how they came into possession of the coin. We do know, and we believe we can prove it. Let the government take their case to court like anyone else." Gerald sounded extremely convincing, and Timothy held his breath, waiting to see what the judge would say.

The judge handed the piece of paper back to the man with the agents. "There seems to be a genuine question to be decided here. If you want the coin, then you need to take it to court." The judge left the courtroom, and Gerald turned toward them with a smile.

"Who is that guy?" Timothy asked.

"He's the US Attorney," Joiner whispered, and he stood up. Timothy did as well, as they waited for Gerald.

"Can we find another judge?" one of the agents asked as they passed, and the attorney shook his head. "I'll file suit tomorrow morning." They passed out of the room, and Timothy and Joiner fell in behind Gerald as he led them toward the front of the building.

"I'm going to head back to the office," Gerald told them. "Do you need a ride?"

"I'll take Timothy to get his car," Joiner said, and Timothy followed him to the parking garage.

Timothy rode with Joiner, barely able to take his eyes off him. "That was a win," Joiner said as they rode. "I think the agents thought getting the order was a slam dunk."

Timothy nodded, feeling a bit relieved. "How?" To him they hadn't won anything, just delayed. Timothy just saw this as delaying the inevitable, and he was beginning to regret going down this path at all. He should have simply kept the coin in the safe-deposit box and said nothing at all. But that seemed like cheating to him. The coin had been Grampy's and it now belonged to him.

Joiner glanced at him from behind the wheel. "Because now the government has to sue you, and they'll be on the defensive. As long as we actually have the coin, we keep the upper hand. In all the other cases, the government had seized the coins and people were trying to get them returned. This puts us in a position of strength."

Timothy nodded slowly. "Am I stupid for doing this?"

"No, you're not. Sure, you could have kept the coin to yourself like Gerald said earlier, but you couldn't show it to anyone, not safely, and you certainly could never sell it."

"I don't want to sell it." For some unexplainable reason, that coin had become a symbol of his relationship with his grandfather, a link to his grandfather's past and visible proof of the stories that Grampy had told him throughout his entire life. "It's like a link to Grampy."

"I know. I think I understand that now. But your grandfather saved all those coins for you so you could have a better life. He didn't give them to your mother; he hid them for you. I'm not saying you should sell it, but nothing can take away your memories of your grandfather."

"I just miss him," Timothy said around the lump in his throat. Sometimes he felt like such a baby, missing his grandfather and all, but with Grampy he knew he was loved unconditionally, and he desperately missed it. His mother obviously never had. Damn it! Why did everything come back to her?

"You okay?" Joiner asked him, and Timothy realized he must have seen his expression.

"Yeah," he lied. He didn't feel all right at all. Everything felt all messed up and twisted inside him. Joiner pulled into the parking lot and parked right next to Timothy's car.

"I still have a few things to do. I should be home about six. Do you want me to come over?" Joiner asked, and Timothy shook his head.

"Could I come to your place?" Timothy asked.

"Of course. I'll meet you there at about six."

Timothy opened his door to get out but stopped. Leaning over the seat, he touched Joiner's cheek and gave him a kiss. To Timothy's surprise, he deepened it quickly. It felt like a door inside him that had been closed for a long time opened, allowing the pent-up anger and fear that he'd been carrying around with him for so very long to escape. Timothy's head felt light, and he shifted on the seat, pressing against Joiner.

A honking horn brought him back to reality, and Timothy shifted back onto the seat with a sheepish grin. "Sorry, I got carried away." Timothy could feel his face flushing, and he refused to look as the other car wove around them.

"Don't be sorry," Joiner told him with a grin. "You never need to be sorry for kissing me, except maybe if you try to do it in the office. Although there is a rumor, more like office legend, I guess, that Gerald was once caught kissing Dieter in one of the conference rooms." Timothy chuckled as he opened his car door and got out. He saw Joiner wave before he closed the door, and Joiner slowly pulled away. Timothy got into his car and drove to his apartment.

Once he got home, Timothy booted up his home computer and logged into work so he could try to catch up on some of the work he'd missed. His supervisor had been very understanding, and Timothy didn't want to be seen as taking advantage. He worked until it was time for him to leave. Pleased with his progress, Timothy shut down his laptop and hurried out of the house before driving to Joiner's.

He parked out front, and Joiner seemed to be waiting for him. Timothy got out of the car, and Joiner met him halfway up the walk. "I just got home. Do you want to get some dinner?"

"Can we order a pizza?" Timothy asked, as Joiner led him inside. As soon as the door closed, Timothy was all over Joiner. He heard a thud as Joiner bumped back against the door. Joiner returned his kisses with a fervor that equaled all the desire and pent-up energy that swirled like a hurricane inside Timothy.

"What's this?" Joiner asked when they came up for air. "Not that I'm complaining, but I...."

Timothy looked Joiner in the eye. "Things just clicked for me, I guess," Timothy began as he pressed himself to Joiner, relishing his heat and the feel of his hands on his back. "I never realized how much I'd been living in fear and shame. After what my mother did and then Dale's rejection, I kept myself locked away." Timothy searched Joiner's eyes for reassurance. "After I told you, I still expected a rejection, even after you were so nice to me. But you didn't. You've been there, and I guess it's time I stopped living in the past."

"Are you sure?" Joiner asked, and instead of answering, Timothy showed him. Leaning forward, he took Joiner's lips. He felt Joiner holding back, and then Joiner tightened his arms around him, and Joiner deepened the kiss, taking charge. Timothy practically vibrated with excitement when he felt Joiner move one of his hands beneath his shirt, stroking the bare skin of his back, and every time Joiner touched him, it sent a jolt of electricity straight to his cock. Timothy had been dead, or at least he'd felt dead, and now he was on fire and his heart pounded in his chest like it never had before. For years, he'd hidden away in fear. Timothy realized he hadn't been living, but now he felt truly alive.

"Can we go somewhere more comfortable?" Joiner asked once they came up for air, and Timothy nodded, feeling too breathless to form words. Joiner took his hand and led him up the stairs and into his bedroom. The room was familiar, but it felt so different from the other night. Then, he'd been afraid, even of Joiner, but now that was gone. When Joiner pulled him close, Timothy felt his excitement begin to build. Ever since he'd been taken by force, for Timothy, sex has been something he feared. Timothy always wondered how he would feel having someone else touch him, but with Joiner, he knew it would be okay, and the nervousness he was afraid he'd feel didn't materialize.

Joiner closed the bedroom door with his foot without stopping the intensely deep kissing. Timothy felt Joiner's hands under his shirt, and when Joiner lifted the fabric, Timothy stretched his arms. The kisses paused just long enough for Joiner to pull off his shirt, and then Joiner's lips and tongue were back, tasting him deeply. Timothy's head spun, and he held on to Joiner's shoulder, trying to steady himself.

Timothy was completely unprepared for the burst of sensation when he felt Joiner's thumbs pluck lightly at each of his nipples. Timothy hissed softly, and Joiner kissed him harder. The bed hit the back of Timothy's legs, the first indication he was aware of that they'd moved, and Joiner guided him down onto the mattress. Joiner shifted his lips from Timothy's lips to the skin of his chest, and Timothy felt rather than heard himself making all kinds of small sounds that he couldn't stop from escaping his lips. "Make all the noise you want," Joiner told him between licks and kisses that trailed over his skin. "There's nothing sexier than the sound of a man when he's being made love to."

Timothy swallowed. That was the first time Joiner had used the "L" word. Timothy tried to remember the last time anyone had used the word "love" in reference to him, and he realized it had to have been Grampy, and that was before he'd really begun to go downhill mentally. Timothy felt like he was sinking, or floating, he wasn't quite sure which, but it felt as though the last supports he'd built in his life had been kicked out from under him, and he waited, expecting to hit the emotional ground hard, but he didn't. "Is that how you feel?" Timothy asked, almost afraid of the answer.

Joiner looked up, meeting Timothy's eyes in a deep, penetrating gaze that smoldered with desire and want in a way Timothy nearly didn't recognize because these things were so new to him. "That's exactly how I feel." Joiner shifted, and in an instant, he was kissing him again. Timothy's legs still dangled off the side of the bed, and Joiner lifted them and then settled on top of him, trailing hot hands down his skin as Timothy was kissed within an inch of his life. "Scoot up," Joiner told him under his breath, and Timothy moved back onto the bed. "I want to see all of you," Joiner said, and Timothy felt Joiner working open his belt. Timothy fumbled with Joiner's clothes at the same time, wanting desperately to touch. Shifting on the bed, Joiner stood up, and Timothy watched with rapt attention as Joiner pulled off his shirt. Joiner rocked back and forth, taking off his shoes, and then he opened his pants, stepping out of them. Timothy watched Joiner, wearing only a pair of black briefs, crawl back onto the bed like a prowling panther. Timothy raised his hips, and Joiner tugged off his pants, throwing them onto the floor before pressing him into the mattress.

The kissing and caressing began again, this time in much more earnest as Timothy flexed his hips, Joiner's length sliding against Timothy's. He'd done this before, with Dale in college, and it had felt good then, so Timothy was prepared when Joiner touched him. What he wasn't prepared for was the amazing sensation when Joiner slid his hand beneath the waistband of his briefs, and wrapped those incredible fingers tightly around his length. Timothy thought he was going to come right then and there. "Hasn't anyone ever touched you before?" Joiner asked, and Timothy nodded quickly.

"A few times in college, but...." He trailed off. Now was not the time to discuss what he and Dale had done, especially not with Joiner stroking his cock so freaking perfectly that Timothy thought Joiner might be able to read his mind to know exactly what he wanted.

"So it's been a long time," Joiner said with a mischievous grin, and before Timothy could answer, Joiner sucked him deep. No one had ever done that before, and Timothy had dreamed what it would feel like to have someone suck him. Never in his wildest dreams did he imagine it would feel like this. He was inside Joiner, surrounded by the hottest wetness ever. Timothy's head began to throb, and he could feel his cock jumping already.

"Joiner, I'm...." Timothy felt his excitement building already, and he tried to hold it back, but he couldn't. Joiner sucked harder, and Timothy came, still trying to hold back the tide of his excitement. Breathing like a runner, Timothy opened his eyes and saw Joiner as his cock slid from between Joiner's lips. The words were on the tip of his tongue to apologize, but Joiner kissed them away almost before Timothy could open his mouth.

His body felt like Jell-O, and once he caught his breath, Timothy reached to the waistband of Joiner's black briefs, sliding his hand under the fabric, cupping the other man's hard butt. "I want to make you feel the same way," Timothy said as he heard Joiner moan softly.

Joiner lifted himself and rolled onto his back. Timothy sat up and looked down at Joiner. He didn't know where to start. Other than his own body, he'd only been with one other person, and they hadn't done enough for him to really have much experience. "Simply do what you like. You can't go wrong, I promise," Joiner said.

Shoving his timidity aside, Timothy reached out and stroked the skin of Joiner's chest. He wanted it all. Whatever it was, Timothy wanted to experience everything. He'd kept himself locked away behind walls of his own making for so long that with them gone, he felt free. Timothy tasted Joiner's skin, licking around one of his small, firm nipples. Joiner's skin tasted slightly salty and warm with a hint of something unique that he expected was all Joiner. As he licked across Joiner's stomach, he felt and heard Joiner giggle, muscles fluttering beneath his tongue. Unable to wait anymore, Timothy sat back on his knees and pulled back Joiner's briefs. The bulge had been big, but when he tugged away the fabric, Joiner's cock jumped to meet him. Timothy stroked along the length the way Joiner had for him, and he watched as Joiner reacted, eyes closing, breath hissing between clenched teeth. "Is this okay?"

"It's perfect," Joiner told him, and Timothy stroked harder before doing what Joiner had, taking him into his mouth. Timothy hadn't known what to expect, but he hadn't anticipated the heady, strong taste of his lover, or the way Joiner felt on his tongue. "Be careful and relax," Joiner encouraged him, and Timothy took him deep before backing off quickly and then trying again more slowly and carefully. After a few minutes, he seemed to get the hang of it, at least that was what he thought by the sounds Joiner was making. "God, Timmy!" Joiner cried out, and Timothy cupped Joiner's balls as his confidence grew with each cry.

Timothy loved that he was the one that Joiner was making these sounds for. He had never realized that the best turn-on could be making someone else happy. Timothy could feel himself getting hard again as Joiner thrust slightly beneath him. Letting him fall from his lips, Timothy kissed Joiner hard. Before he knew it, Joiner had rolled them on the bed, his weight on top of Timothy, kissing as they both frantically ground their bodies against one another. Joiner's cock slid against his, and they kissed, Joiner holding his butt to put more pressure between them. "Is this okay?" Joiner asked between gritted teeth, and Timothy nodded before Joiner kissed him again.

Timothy could barely answer, though he managed to nod. How could he ever have imagined that something as simple as rubbing against another person could feel so danged amazing? Timothy could already feel his climax building, and Joiner's movements and breathing became erratic. Joiner cried out softly, and Timothy felt warmth spread between them. As Timothy watched Joiner come, the sight of his lover's wide eyes and even wider mouth sent Timothy over the edge as well.

Joiner held him tight, and Timothy listened to the sound of their breathing for quite a while, enjoying the weight and feel of Joiner's body against his. "I love this," Timothy said softly, and Joiner lifted his head off Timothy's shoulder, looking into his eyes. "No one's held me in a very long time." Timothy closed his eyes and held his breath, releasing it slowly as the realization hit him that the last person who'd given him a hug out of true emotion was Grampy.

"Am I hurting you?" Joiner asked, and Timothy felt Joiner lightly brush his hand across Timothy's forehead.

"No. It's just hard to explain."

Joiner nodded slowly. "Actually, it's not. You've been hurt pretty badly by people who should have loved and treasured you. You keep waiting for me to hurt you just like everyone else has." Joiner rolled off him onto the mattress. "I won't, at least not on purpose." Joiner got up and hurried to the bathroom, returning with a towel that he used to clean them both up before lying next to him on the bed once again. "Can I ask you something?" Timothy nodded and looked intently into Joiner's deep eyes. "When was the last time you were touched by someone who loved you?"

Timothy felt a lump forming in his throat. "A couple years ago, Grampy was lucid and I hugged him. He hugged me back. After that he wasn't able to again."

"When was the last time anyone said they loved you?" Joiner asked, and Timothy had to think about it.

"About the same time, I guess." Timothy thought hard. He knew the only person to say they loved him since he'd left home was Grampy. "I think it was the same visit. Why?"

"No reason, other than it's been too long." Joiner touched his cheek, stroking his hand over the late-day stubble, tickling a little. "I meant what I said earlier. We were making love." Joiner leaned over him, kissing him sweetly and deeply. The earnestness from earlier was gone, replaced by feelings that were much deeper. Joiner cupped Timothy's head, and the kiss deepened and became more passionate. Timothy knew what Joiner was feeling because every bit of it came through that kiss, the same way Timothy let his emotions flow right back. He couldn't make himself say the words, not yet, but he could let Joiner feel them, and he did.

Joiner held and kissed him for quite a while. Timothy lost all track of time, and that was perfectly fine with him because there was no place he wanted to be other than in Joiner's arms. Eventually, their stomachs began to voice their own opinions, and Timothy smiled when Joiner rolled over on the bed and fished his cell phone out of his pants. Timothy heard him order a pizza and then close the phone.

Timothy didn't want to move, and he was trying to figure out how to get Joiner to feed him pizza in bed when he figured they had both better get up or the pizza delivery guy was going to get quite a surprise when he opened the door.

By the time the doorbell rang, they'd been sitting in Joiner's living room for a few minutes curled together on the sofa, ignoring the television in favor of necking like teenagers. Joiner got the pizza and returned with a smile on his face. He set the box on the table and got some plates and bottles of beer before sitting on the sofa again.

Half an hour later, they'd polished off enough pepperoni and cheese to feed a small army, and Timothy had curled against Joiner, his eyes drooping closed from plenty of food and everything else. Timothy's phone rang, and he fished it out of his pocket, checking the display. He only answered it because Joiner groaned, and he wanted to silence the thing.

"Mr. Besch?" a woman's voice inquired.

"Yes, who's calling?" Timothy immediately stiffened, wondering what this call was about.

"I'm Helen Marsh from St. Mary's Hospital. Your mother is one of our patients, and she's been asking for you." She sounded so clinical.

Timothy nearly hung up the phone without saying anything, but he felt Joiner's arms around him. "I don't have anything to say to her."

"Mr. Besch, your mother may not survive. When she arrived, she had multiple injuries, and they were complicated by all the drugs in her system. We don't know how she will respond to treatment, and her prognosis isn't good. But she's been lucid some of the time, and you're the only person she's asked for." There was a hint of pleading in her voice that Timothy didn't expect. "This may be your only chance."

Timothy didn't know what to say, and he swallowed hard. "Thank you." Then he disconnected the call and set the phone on the table.

"What is it?" Joiner asked. "I know it's about your mother."

"She's dying," Timothy said, and Joiner got up, cleaning up the dishes before stepping back into the room to stare at him.

"Aren't you ready to go?"

"Go?"

"To the hospital." Joiner sat on the sofa and began pulling on his shoes. "I know how you feel, and I can't blame you. But she's dying, and you aren't going to get another chance."

"A chance for what? For her to hurt me yet again?" Timothy glared at Joiner and figured that maybe it *was* time to go—for him to go home.

Joiner stood in front of him, but Timothy could not bring himself to look at him. He'd thought Joiner was on his side. Timothy thought he understood, but he didn't. Maybe Joiner was like Dale after all, and didn't believe him, either. "This could be your last opportunity to tell her how you feel." Slowly Timothy lifted his eyes. "Yell at her, call her the 'bitch from hell' if you want, but this could be the last time you get to say anything to her. I don't want you to go for her. I want you to go for *you,* because maybe you can get some closure."

Timothy gaped. He knew his mouth hung open, but he could barely believe he'd heard Joiner correctly. Joiner *did* get it, and for the first time in quite a while, Timothy felt as though he truly had someone on his side. Standing up, he forced himself to pull on his shoes and grab his things before following Joiner to his car.

Timothy stared out the windows as they rode through traffic toward downtown. His thoughts kept playing over what his mother had done, and Timothy refused to close his eyes, because he could almost feel the hurt and pain welling up again. "I know this is hard," Joiner said from the driver's seat, and Timothy turned his head away from the lights that flashed by.

"That's the understatement of the century," Timothy snarked, and immediately he regretted it. He'd agreed to come, and it wasn't Joiner's fault. "Sorry," he added softly. Joiner didn't try talking again, and Timothy knew he'd hurt him, though he really hadn't meant to. Thankfully, the ride to the hospital wasn't too long, and after Joiner parked the car, Timothy got out and blankly began walking toward the hospital entrance. He jumped slightly when Joiner took his hand, and Timothy squeezed it in return as they approached the entrance.

"I'm sorry, visiting hours are over," the woman behind the desk said as they approached.

"I got a call from Helen Marsh," Timothy began, and those seemed to be the magic words, because she began typing in her computer. "The patient's name is Julie Besch."

"Yes. ICU is on the third floor. Mrs. Marsh is on duty, and she can take it from there. The elevators are just around the corner," she said quietly, as though a sleeping patient were in the room with her.

Timothy let Joiner lead him to the elevator, and they rode to the third floor, following the signs to Intensive Care. As they approached the desk, Timothy told the woman his name, and she asked him to wait a minute. Timothy looked around and then at Joiner. He wanted more than anything to just leave and go home. He did not want to see his mother or talk to her—she'd already caused him enough pain.

Timothy was just about to turn around to leave when he felt Joiner's hand on his back, lightly touching him, and Timothy was reminded that he wasn't alone. Joiner was with him. Turning his head, he looked into his lover's eyes and saw nothing but very determined support.

"Mr. Besch, I'm Helen. Thank you for coming," the nurse who had called him said and led them quietly down a darkened hallway toward the very end room. "The last I checked she was asleep, which is good." Timothy felt his breath shorten as they got closer to his mother's room.

"What's wrong with her?" Timothy asked once they stopped outside the open door. He didn't look inside.

"As I said on the phone, she has internal injuries that seem to be consistent with being kicked, along with what appears to be a long history of drug use," Helen said, glancing into the room. "Unfortunately, it's the two of them combined that are making her condition worse. Her body is trying to heal from the injuries, but the drugs in her system are preventing that. We've tried to keep her as comfortable as we can, but as the drugs are leaving her system, the withdrawal symptoms are quite strong. She is restrained for her own protection."

Timothy nodded. He'd seen and felt what his mother would do to get a fix when she needed one. Helen looked into the room and motioned for Timothy to go inside. Timothy got as far as the doorway and then stopped, looking at his mother lying in the hospital bed. She looked so small and frail with the tubes and machines around her. "When I was young, she was a great mother," Timothy said softly. "I can remember her taking me to school, and we used to go places together with Grampy." Timothy turned to Joiner. "We used to go to the movies together, just the two of us, on a Saturday afternoon." Timothy was trying to remember the good times and forget where he was. "When I was twelve, she packed Grampy and me in the car, and we drove out to South Dakota. We played games the entire way there and back."

"That person is still there," Helen said, and he turned to her, his anger threatening to come to the surface.

"No. That person is gone. She allowed the drugs to take that person away, and to leave me with... with a person who would...." Timothy stopped himself from saying out loud what she'd done. Joiner held him tighter, and Timothy clamped his eyes closed to try to get hold of himself.

"Timmy?" she said, and it sounded like the mother from his long-ago memories, not the woman he'd run away from. "Is that you?"

Timothy watched as his mother's eyes opened and he saw the ghost of a smile form on her lips.

"We've been trying to get the drugs out of her system, and it's left her very weak, but hopefully her mind is clearer now," Helen said from behind him, and Timothy nodded, but did not step further into the room.

"Timmy," his mother said again, and he saw tears running down her cheeks. "You came."

Timothy nodded but said nothing to her. He didn't know what he should or could say. He watched her for a while, and then he felt Joiner press him forward slightly, and Timothy took his first step into the room. Part of him wanted to scream at her; another part wanted to ask her why she'd done what she had done. But as Timothy approached her, he realized he couldn't do either one. So he sat down in a chair across from her and stared at the bed. The woman there was a stranger. She barely looked like the mother he wanted to remember. She was covered in bruises, and Timothy knew that was probably the least of her injuries.

"You came," she said over and over, and Timothy realized she was falling asleep.

"We're trying to keep her sedated so her body can work to get rid of the drugs. We've already operated once, and we need to again, but the doctors don't want to do that until she's stabilized," Helen said, and Timothy nodded his understanding.

Standing up, Timothy sniffled once and then approached the bed. His mother's eyes were closed now, and she looked deeply asleep. "I just want to know what happened," he said softly. Sleeping or not, Timothy knew he had to say what he'd come here to say. "What was it that drove you away from us and into drugs? What did I do to make you want to leave me?"

Timothy felt the tears begin, and he let them come. Joiner took one of Timothy's hands in his and held it as Timothy continued. "The drugs became more important than me. Do you remember any of it?" He didn't expect an answer, and his mother's eyes remained closed and she didn't move. "You destroyed our family and our lives for the drugs, and you made me hate you. I still do. I hate what you became, and I hate what you let happen to me, because whether you meant it, Mama, you let some man rape me so you could get a fix." Timothy heard Helen gasp, and felt Joiner tighten his grip on him. "I was eighteen years old, and you need a goddamned fix so badly that you gave me to your dealer in exchange for drugs. He raped me and hurt me so badly I thought I was going to die."

Timothy's voice faltered, and he looked at Joiner, who nodded in encouragement. "You nearly destroyed my life, Mama, all because of the fucking drugs. I spent years wondering what I'd done to you to deserve to be treated like that, and it took me a long time to realize I'd done nothing. All the blame and guilt are yours, not mine." Timothy took a deep breath and swiped his hand at the tears on his face. "Well, I hope they were worth it, because I am through with you forever. I will not be back, and live or die, you will never see me again, because I'll be damned if I'm going to give you the opportunity to hurt me ever again." Timothy blinked away the last of the tears and stepped back from the bed. When he looked at Helen, there was no disguising the horror on her face, but Timothy didn't give it much time to register, as he turned and walked out of the room without looking back.

Helen met him in the hallway, and she couldn't look him in the eyes. "I'm sorry," she said softly. "I didn't know."

Timothy took a deep, cleansing breath and let it out slowly. "You couldn't have. But I want to thank you. I was able to say what I needed to."

"I think I know the answer, but if something happens, do you want to be notified?" Helen asked, and Timothy saw her pull a tissue out of her pocket and dab her eyes.

"No. My mother has been dead for quite a long time. I think I realize that now." Timothy turned and walked back down the hallway toward the elevator. He heard Joiner behind him. They said nothing, but as soon as the elevator doors slid closed with them inside, Joiner pulled Timothy to him, hugging tight.

"I'm sorry I pushed you into this," Joiner said with tears in his voice.

"You were right," Timothy muttered into Joiner's neck. "I needed to tell her. Even if she couldn't understand, I needed to say it." A ding indicated they had reached the hospital lobby. "And I was mad at you for making me feel guilty for not wanting to come, but it was the right thing." The doors slid open, and Joiner continued holding him for a few seconds. Then they stepped out of the elevator, walking out of the hospital and directly to Joiner's car.

They didn't speak much, and Timothy noticed that Joiner took him back to his place, which made sense, since that's where his car was. But Timothy wasn't thinking very well, and once they arrived, he let Joiner lead him up the walk and inside the apartment. He expected Joiner to take him to his bedroom, but instead, they went into the living room. Timothy sat down, and Joiner left, returning a few minutes later with a bottle of something clear and two shot glasses. "I'd say you earned a few belts."

Timothy didn't drink much hard liquor, but when Joiner offered him the glass, he took it and threw it back, closing his eyes at the bite before handing the glass to Joiner for another. Timothy drank that one as well before settling back on the sofa. The warmth spread from his stomach to the rest of his body, and Timothy let his mind float as the alcohol dulled his anxious nerves. Joiner pointed to the bottle, and Timothy shook his head. That was enough. Joiner capped the bottle and carried it away.

When he returned, Joiner held out his hand, and Timothy let himself be led to Joiner's bedroom. Without saying a word, Joiner stripped off Timothy's clothes and helped him climb into bed. The last thing Timothy remembered about that night was Joiner holding him close, and how quiet his mind felt.

CHAPTER 6

JOINER loved waking up next to Timothy. What he hated was that they had places they needed to be, and after the night Timothy had had, Joiner wished they could do nothing but stay in bed, but both of them had to go to work. So after he checked the clock, Joiner turned off the alarm and carefully got out of bed. Letting Timothy sleep, he quietly went into the bathroom and got cleaned up before returning to the bedroom. Timothy was almost completely burrowed under the covers, and Joiner leaned over the bed, waking him up with small kisses on Timothy's cheek. "Sweetheart, we need to go to work." Timothy groaned loudly and rolled over, so Joiner climbed beneath the covers, and Timothy burrowed next to him. "We have to go to work."

Timothy groaned again, but after a few minutes, they got out of bed. While Timothy dressed, Joiner made a quick breakfast, and after kissing him goodbye, they left the apartment, and Joiner drove to his office.

It was still early when he arrived, but Gerald's light was on when he walked by. "Joiner," Gerald called, and he went into the office.

"Morning, Gerald," Joiner said as he sat where Gerald indicated.

Gerald looked at him intently, and Joiner knew instantly there was nothing remotely social about why he'd been called in here. "Last evening I got a call from the US Attorney's Office. It seems our little tactic yesterday got the attention of some of his supervisors in Washington, and they do not like to lose. He told me as a courtesy that they were going to the court of appeals for an order to turn over the coin on the grounds of national security. They use that for everything these days because politically it gives them carte blanche to do what they want and they don't have to explain. I need you to see if we can get some time with Timothy today."

"Why would the US Attorney tell you?" Joiner asked. "Not that I'm questioning you, but I want to understand."

Gerald nodded slowly. "Respect and common courtesy. We may have beaten him yesterday, but we did it fair and square. His supervisors aren't playing fair. By the way, we aren't having this conversation, just like I never talked to him last night. Now, I have some calls to make. Let me know what Timothy says." Gerald picked up the phone, and Joiner left the office, not relishing the call he was going to have to make.

Joiner turned on the light and sat at his desk. Checking his watch, he figured Timothy wasn't at work yet, so he booted up his computer and got to work. At eight o'clock, he knew he couldn't put it off any longer, so Joiner picked up the phone and called Timothy.

"Timothy Besch."

"It's Joiner. Gerald asked me to call." Joiner told Timothy what Gerald had told him. "Is it possible for you to come to the office?"

"I suppose I can be there at four," Timothy said, and Joiner heard the defeated tone in his voice. "Should I stop by the deposit box on the way?"

"I'll ask Gerald, but I doubt it. He has something he's working on—I can see it in his eyes." Joiner was trying to make Timothy feel better, but he knew he wasn't doing a good job. To Timothy, that coin wasn't money or gold but a link to his grandfather, the one person who'd always loved him, and now someone was trying to take it away. He could almost see the hurt look on Timothy's face.

"Okay, I'll be there," Timothy said so softly Joiner could barely hear him, and then the connection ended. Joiner stared at the phone for a few seconds before hanging it up. Gerald was at his door almost as soon as the phone hit the cradle. "Timothy will be here at four," Joiner told him.

"Good. I want you to authenticate the story that Timothy told us yesterday. Get anything you can to corroborate that story. Find out when Timothy's family moved to Milwaukee. Get me everything you can, and fast," Gerald said with a burst of energy. "Call me on my cell—I have to get to the federal building, and I need it when I get back." Gerald was gone before Joiner could ask any questions.

Joiner wanted to call Timothy back to make sure he was okay, but he knew the best thing he could do to help was to get the information Gerald requested, so he got to work. Joiner had written down the story as Timothy had told it, so he began with weather reports, and found that there was indeed a hot spell where temperatures hit the midnineties for two days in April of 1933. That part was easy. But finding out the details about the mint itself took some additional time, as did locating the information on Timothy's family.

His phone rang, and Joiner jumped before answering it. "Come to my office," Gerald said and then hung up. Joiner grabbed his notepad, locked his computer, and hurried down the hall. He was surprised to see Agent Forrester sitting in one of Gerald's guest chairs. Gerald motioned Joiner toward one of the others. "I'm going to cut to the chase, Agent Forrester. The coin in question does not belong to the US Government. We truly believe the coin belongs to my client."

"None of those coins were ever issued, so they remain the property of the government," Agent Forrester said in a level voice.

"Unless the government used it as payment," Gerald explained, and Joiner saw Agent Forrester's eyes widen as the implication of what he'd just heard sank in. "I know this isn't your decision to make. You need to follow your directives; I know that."

"Then why did you invite me here?" Agent Forrester asked, even though he didn't look surprised at all.

"I'd like you to deliver a message for me. I'd like to have someone who can make decisions here at four fifteen today, along with the US Attorney. I have a proposal that can save everyone a lot of time, money, and effort."

"I can't make any promises," Agent Forrester said.

Gerald leaned forward slightly in his chair. "Tell them this. It will not look good on anyone's record if the government wrongly seizes an asset of an American citizen, especially if that seizure occurs in front of every news camera in town." Gerald stared hard at Agent Forrester, and Joiner had to stop the chuckle that threatened to boil up. Instead, he kept his expression even.

To his credit, Agent Forrester didn't ask anything, he simply stood up and walked toward the door. "I'll deliver your message." Agent Forrester left, and Joiner waited until Gerald had shut the door before telling him everything he'd found out. When Joiner was done, Gerald simply nodded like he was telling him what he already knew.

"You did a great job," Gerald told him as he stood. He'd expected more instructions from him, but Gerald returned to his desk.

"Can I ask what you have planned?" Joiner desperately wanted to understand what was running through Gerald's mind.

"Not right now, but bring Timothy back when he gets here, and I'll explain everything to both of you." Gerald sat at his desk chair, and Joiner took that as his dismissal, leaving the office to return to his own. Gerald clearly had something planned, and knowing his boss, it would definitely be interesting.

JOINER worked, head down, the rest of the day. Brian gave him a ton of research to do, and thankfully that kept him so occupied that he didn't have time to worry about what was going to happen later, although he did find that Timothy was never far from his thoughts. A few times, he wondered what Timothy must be thinking. If Joiner was worried about whatever Gerald had planned, then Timothy must be going out of his mind. At lunch, he thought about calling Timothy, but he had nothing to tell him, and that would only make things worse for his lover, so he did nothing and waited.

When his phone finally rang just before four o'clock, he told the receptionist to send Timothy back to his office, and when Timothy walked into his tiny work space, Joiner hurried to him, and after closing the door, hugged Timothy tight before kissing him hard. There were many things that had surprised him since meeting Timothy, but the one that most took him by surprise was how much the line between lover and client was blurring for him. When he'd first met Timothy, he thought he could keep the case separate from his feelings, but he was now having a difficult time doing just that. When Gerald had told him about what the attorneys were doing, he hadn't thought in terms of the case, but in terms of Timothy and how he would feel. "Are you okay?" Joiner asked, still holding on to him.

"I guess so. Do you know anything?" Timothy's head rested in his shoulder.

"Not much, but we will soon," Joiner answered. "I did a lot of research, and Gerald asked me to fact-check the story your grandfather told you, but other than that, he didn't tell me what he has planned." Joiner could feel the uncertainty and worry radiating off Timothy.

"Do you think I'm being stupid? Holding on to a coin like this— it's just a bit of shiny metal. It's not as though it will bring Grampy back to me."

"Is that how you feel?" Joiner asked, releasing him from the hug.

Timothy shook his head. "No. It's more than that somehow."

"In my research, I found out that many people believe that the 1933 Double Eagle has almost talismanic powers. It's probably bunk, but maybe for you this one does, who's to say? Besides, no one should have the right to take what isn't theirs, and that goes for the government as well as anyone else." Joiner felt very strongly about that.

"Is that why you became an attorney?"

"No. I became an attorney because I thought I could make a lot of money at it. But then I met Gerald. He's so passionate about what he does. He helps people because he believes in them, and I swear he would do what he does for free because it's what he loves, and I think I'm starting to understand how that feels." Joiner wasn't sure if he was making sense, but he could feel that his whole attitude toward the law was shifting, and he knew that was because of Gerald, and Timothy, as well. "We need to get to Gerald's office; he'll explain what he has in mind."

Timothy opened the door, and Joiner led him to Gerald's office, where they both went inside and closed the door. "We don't have much time before the others arrive, and I don't want to keep them waiting." Gerald motioned toward the chairs. "I have an idea, which I put into motion without speaking with you because I had to move fast," Gerald told Timothy. "What I'm going to propose is a sort of arbitration. A court case could go on for years and get extremely expensive."

"I don't understand," Timothy said.

"I know. What's been bothering me the whole time is that cases like this drag on for years, and I don't want you to spend your grandfather's legacy trying to keep your grandfather's legacy, and that could easily happen." Gerald sat down next to Timothy.

"I trust you, Gerald," Timothy said and then turned to Joiner. "I trust both of you."

Joiner felt his throat close a little as he realized how monumental that was for Timothy. Most of the people in his life had betrayed him. It felt like Timothy was giving him a precious gift.

"Thank you," Gerald said. "We won't let you down. We may not win, but both of us will do our very best for you."

A soft knock sounded on the door. "The people you were expecting are here. I put them in the conference room," Annette, Gerald's assistant, explained and then closed the door. Gerald stood up, and the three of them walked together to the room.

Gerald and Timothy walked in first, and Joiner followed behind. The people already waiting in the room stood up, and Gerald and Timothy took their places side by side, while Joiner sat further down the table. Agent Forrester made introductions. "This is Secret Service Regional Director Stanley Howards and Deputy US Attorney Simon Bellows."

Gerald stood and shook hands. "Gerald Young, and my client, Timothy Besch. Also my associate, Joiner Carver." Joiner and Timothy both shook hands with each of them before settling in their chairs.

"Can you tell me what it is you have planned? Agent Forrester delivered your message, and you can't possibly think we'll allow you to do as you suggested."

Gerald remained calm, even though Timothy looked nervous as hell, and Joiner wished he'd been able to sit next to him, but it wouldn't have been appropriate. "I most certainly would, and you know it. As soon as we received an order to turn over the coin, our first call would be to CNN and everyone else. These coins have become rather famous lately, and you know how the government would look seizing something from a man as young and innocent-looking as my client. The press would have a feeding frenzy, especially when it comes to light that that coin is one of the few things left to Mr. Besch by his grandfather."

Joiner saw even the US Attorney looked uncomfortable. "So what are you proposing?"

"You arrange for a specialized arbitration hearing presided over by a mutually agreed upon retired federal judge. You present your case, and we'll present ours. No playing to a jury, and neither of us has to wait years to get an answer."

"You'll turn over the object in question at that time?"

"If after the hearing the ruling is in your favor, yes," Gerald answered. "No media and no fanfare. However, I will caution all of you. If there is so much as a hint that you are abusing your position or not playing fair, I will alert the media so fast it'll make your heads spin. And I'll make sure they have your full names." Gerald was playing tough, and as Joiner looked over the faces of the men in the room, they still seemed skeptical. "It's very simple, gentlemen. You can save yourself and the taxpayers a great deal of time and money, or you can drag this out for years. Also, if the case is settled without official court records, your precedents stay intact and you don't have prior cases coming back to haunt you. It's your call."

The regional director looked at the other men, and Joiner could see he was thinking pretty hard. "I want this kept quiet," the regional director said firmly.

"It will be, as long as you keep up your end of the bargain," Gerald said, and that was when Joiner knew they were going to go for it. He wasn't sure how happy he was about the whole thing, but Gerald was probably right: a long fight would probably be something Timothy couldn't afford.

"Who pays for this?" the regional director asked.

"You do," Gerald answered. "After all, you're the ones trying to seize my client's property." Joiner had never seen Gerald with so cold an expression on his face. Joiner knew he was sending a message to the director that he felt very strongly about this.

The director swallowed, and Joiner saw a hint of annoyance on his face, but he knew when he was bested and that anything he did other than agree was going to make him look very bad. "Very well. We'll agree to your proposal." The regional director stood up. "I assume you and the US Attorney can work out the details?" When they both nodded, Director Howard left the room, and Joiner saw Annette escorting both him and Agent Forrester toward the reception area.

Gerald and Bellows went back and forth negotiating the details of the hearing, but after an hour, they had reached an agreement. Once they were done, the US Attorney left as well, and Gerald slumped back into his chair, taking a huge breath.

Timothy actually spoke for the first time since they'd stepped into the room. "I take it that went well."

"I think so. The hearing will be in a few weeks," Gerald explained. "I know there was a lot of back and forth, but basically we'll meet in a neutral location with a judge that we both agree on. We'll put together a list of candidates, and they'll do the same. Then, at the hearing, we'll each present our argument, and the retired judge will decide. It's that simple, and we've both agreed to let this be the final word. So if we win, you get to keep the coin, but if we lose, we've given up the right to appeal. Can you live with that?"

Timothy stood up and began pacing through the room. "I don't think I have a choice. I can't afford a long fight. I said I trusted you, and I do." Timothy stopped walking and turned to Gerald, holding out his hand. "Thank you."

"You're welcome," Gerald said with a smile, and he left the conference room.

Joiner wasn't quite sure how to read Timothy's expression. "I don't know how I'm supposed to feel right now," Timothy explained.

"Look at it this way: in a few weeks, you'll know one way or another. There won't be a cloud of uncertainty hanging over you," Joiner said as he reached out to take Timothy's hand. "I'd go home with you now, but I have this case I'm doing for someone really special and I've got to get to work on it." Joiner winked, and Timothy smiled. "I'll see you tonight, though."

"Okay. I've got some projects to do at the house, so stop by, and we can go from there." Timothy kissed him lightly, and then Joiner gathered his papers before ushering Timothy out of the building. He actually waited until the elevator doors closed before returning to his office.

"Joiner," Gerald called as Joiner passed his office, and he stepped inside. "This hearing is going to move up the timeline on Timothy's case immensely. I need you to look over everything we have, and I want to meet with you at nine tomorrow morning so we can go over everything we need."

"Of course. I have some ideas already that I want to look into, and I'll try to have that by nine as well," Joiner said. He knew there were still major holes in their case that they needed to fill. He just wasn't quite sure how to do it. Gerald simply smiled and nodded. Instead of going to his office, Joiner went directly to the library and got to work.

Joiner worked late, and he wasn't sure Timothy would still be at his house, but he stopped by there first and saw lights on. Walking to the door, he knocked. Timothy opened it a few moments later, all smiles, and it wasn't a second before Joiner had his arms filled with Timothy's warmth. "What's gotten into you? Not that I'm complaining," Joiner said with a small chuckle as Timothy pulled him inside.

"I just missed you, and I realized you were right. No matter what, it will be over soon, and with you and Gerald working together, I can't lose." Timothy sounded so happy that Joiner couldn't bring himself to tell him that there were still major pieces of information that he couldn't seem to find. "What is it?" Timothy asked, and Joiner smiled, reminding himself that this was probably one of those times when he needed to keep the case and his relationship with Timothy separate.

"Nothing," Joiner answered, and he let Timothy lead him inside. The house still smelled like paint, and Joiner realized why: Timothy had finished painting the hallways.

"I'm all done. Every room has been cleaned and painted except the kitchen, and I've made another decision." Timothy paused and Joiner waited for his news. "I've decided to keep the house." Timothy was so excited that Joiner couldn't help letting go of some of the concerns he had about the case and getting into the spirit.

"So what did you have in mind for tonight?" Joiner asked, and Timothy walked over to the pocket door to the dining room, which Joiner now noticed was closed. Timothy pushed it open and revealed what looked like a small table all set for two.

"How did you do this?" Joiner asked as he wandered into the room. "You didn't have anything in the house." Joiner looked at the table. "This is beautiful."

"I found it all in the attic. It was Grammy's. I've decided to bring down and use what I can, and I thought I would start tonight." Timothy moved close, and Joiner pulled him into his arms, kissing Timothy hard.

"You're amazing, you know that?" Joiner kissed him again. "I want you to know that I'm falling in love and I don't want to ever stop." Timothy trembled in his arms. "You don't have to say it back. I just wanted you to know."

Timothy nodded and tilted his head up to meet Joiner's eyes. "I do feel that way about you. It's just so hard to say." Joiner nodded, because he could understand how Timothy felt, regardless of what he said. "I should get dinner," Timothy said, but Joiner wasn't quite ready to let him go just yet. Capturing his lover's lips, he kissed Timothy deeply before following him to the kitchen.

"Can I help?" Joiner asked as wonderful smells surrounded him. Timothy opened the old oven and pulled out an even older roasting pan that must have been his grandmother's. The entire room filled with the scent of roast beef, potatoes, and carrots. It smelled like warmth and home. Timothy transferred the meat to a cutting board and began slicing it. "My mother called just before I left the office," Joiner said. "She asked if I would come for a visit this weekend, and I was wondering if you'd like to come with me."

Timothy stopped moving, his knife stilling in midslice. "You want me to meet your family?" Timothy began working again, and Joiner saw his hand shaking slightly. "Do you think they'll like me?"

"They'll love you. My mother has been hoping I'd settle down for a while, and when I told her about you, she specifically asked to meet you."

"Have you ever brought anyone else home to meet them?" Timothy finished slicing the meat and began adding potatoes and carrots to the plates.

"No, because I've never cared about anyone enough to want to," Joiner answered, and he knew it was true. Timothy was the only person he'd loved enough to have meet his family. "Will you go with me?"

Timothy nodded as he finished filling the plates. "Of course," he said softly. Joiner followed Timothy into the dining room and sat down where Timothy indicated. "It's been a while since I cooked this. Grampy used to love it, and I would make it for him sometimes." Timothy filled the wine glasses and then sat down himself. "I don't cook a lot anymore."

Joiner inhaled, and the warm scent made his stomach rumble. "It smells amazing." Joiner took a small bite, and the flavor burst on his tongue. He must have moaned out loud, because Timothy smiled and then began to eat too. "You'll really come visit my family?"

"Why wouldn't I?" Timothy asked hesitantly. "From what you've told me, your mother seems like an interesting person. Is there something I should know?"

Joiner shook his head. "No. I'm glad you'll come with me." Joiner continued eating and decided he'd let Timothy see for himself. "So who taught you to cook like this?"

"Believe it or not, my mother did. That was before...." Timothy swallowed, and Joiner regretted asking the question. "She was very different before the drugs."

Joiner nodded and fell quiet. He could see Timothy didn't want to talk about his mother at all. Joiner reached across the table and lightly touched Timothy's hand. Joiner smiled, and Timothy returned it, his silent apology accepted, and their conversation fell off as they continued eating. Joiner, a man who was learning to make his living with words, found that in this instance they were an encumbrance, so he remained quiet and did his speaking with his hand, making small swirls on the back of his lover's hand, locking his eyes onto Timothy's, and his heart.

When their plates were empty, Joiner helped Timothy carry them into the kitchen, and together they did the dishes. Something as normal and ordinary as cleaning up took on a special aura. Timothy washed, and at one point, Joiner moved behind him, pressing to Timothy's back and sliding his hands down his arms. The soapy water slipped around their fingers as Joiner entwined his with Timothy's. "I love you," he said softly into Timothy's ear, and Timothy tilted his head back for a kiss. They stood like that until the water began to chill. Timothy finished the dishes, and Joiner dried them. "Do you have dessert?" Joiner asked.

"Yes, it's at your apartment," Timothy answered, and after turning out the lights, they rode to Joiner's together.

THE door to his apartment closed behind them, and Joiner could wait no longer. He'd held Timothy's hand for most of the drive, but now he wanted much more. Pulling Timothy into his arms without bothering to turn on the lights, he followed the scent of Timothy's warm breath to his mouth. He knew he had to be careful not to overwhelm him. They'd kissed and held each other a lot, but Timothy was sometimes skittish when it came to other forms of intimacy, and Joiner had to remind his overanxious body to slow down. He loved Timothy, he'd come to realize that, and he wanted to show him just how much. But he didn't want to scare his new lover, so he kept his kisses as earnestly gentle as his racing blood and heart would allow.

"Let's go to my room," Joiner said after gentling his kiss, and he saw Timothy nod in the dim light.

Taking Timothy's hand, Joiner led them down the hall. "Do you think I'm broken?" Timothy asked, and Joiner stopped midstep.

"No," Joiner said into the darkness, wishing he could see Timothy's face. Joiner forced his feet to move, and he felt Timothy move behind him. In the bedroom, he turned on the light beside the bed. Timothy sat down on the edge of the mattress, looking at his shoes. Joiner knew that look—Timothy made it whenever he was nervous or uncomfortable about something. "What is it?" Joiner asked as he sat next to him, taking Timothy's hand in his.

"You deserve someone better than me," Timothy said softly. "Someone whole."

Joiner thought carefully before he spoke. "Does this have something to do with what happened to you?" Timothy nodded. "What is it that's worrying you? You don't have to be ashamed or scared to tell me."

Timothy lifted his eyes. "I don't know if we can ever have real sex."

"Sweetheart." Joiner smiled as relief washed through him. "Do you remember what we did last time?" Timothy nodded and blushed adorably. "That was real sex." Joiner stroked Timothy's cheek. "Whatever we do together is a reflection of how we feel for each other. Some couples never have anal sex at all."

"But what if you get bored with me?" Timothy looked miserable and scared, and Joiner realized that the silence through dinner that he'd interpreted as quiet companionship was really Timothy worrying about what would happen next.

"I didn't tell you I loved you for sex. I said I loved you because that's how I feel, and I love you for you, all of you. We'll take things as slow as you like and," Joiner said as he nuzzled lightly behind Timothy's ear, "you have to promise me you'll say something if anything bothers you." Timothy nodded, and Joiner lightly ran his tongue behind Timothy's ear. Timothy moaned very softly before bursting into a fit of giggles.

"That tickles," Timothy said, pushing Joiner away playfully.

"I know, but it got you to laugh," Joiner said, and Timothy stood up and began slowly pacing the floor. He'd hoped to take Timothy's mind off of what was worrying him, but it seemed to have backfired, and Timothy seemed more nervous than ever.

"That doesn't solve anything." Timothy's agitation was worse.

"I'm sorry. I wasn't trying to make you feel uncomfortable."

Timothy stopped moving. "I know. Sometimes it comes out of nowhere. I know that being in control helps, but only sometimes." Joiner held out his arms, and Timothy approached him slowly until Joiner could hold him around the waist. He knew Timothy trusted him, at least to a degree, and he knew Timothy cared for him. The problem wasn't Timothy; it was him. That realization hit Joiner hard as he realized he'd been reading a lot of things wrong lately. He'd thought Timothy had cooked dinner as a romantic gesture, and he probably had, but maybe Timothy hadn't necessarily meant it as foreplay. Sometimes dinner was just dinner, and dessert, cuddling. He also realized that since he and Timothy had been intimate, he'd thought everything was okay, but it wasn't. Timothy's fears were still there, and still real— they'd simply been able to bury them for a while.

"What do you want? I'll do whatever makes you comfortable." Joiner lightly stroked Timothy's back.

"For a while, I used to hate being touched by anyone, and I used to have the most god-awful nightmares all the time," Timothy confessed. "Thankfully I don't have them much anymore. When I was at school, I met with a therapist, and she was able to help me a lot. She'd been"—Timothy paused and swallowed—"raped, too, so she didn't look at me funny, and was actually really able to help with a lot of things. The first therapist I went to was one of those 'I'm okay, you're okay' kind of guys, and he was useless. I thought Monica would be the same way, but she wasn't. She was like talking to a big sister who knew exactly what I was going through." Timothy leaned against him, and Joiner continued the light, careful caresses.

"We never have to do anything you don't want," Joiner reiterated. "I'd never want to hurt you."

"I know," Timothy said, and he tilted them back onto the mattress. Timothy kissed him lightly. "I'm just afraid. I spent a lot of years being afraid, and Monica helped me with that too."

"But sex was something she couldn't help you with," Joiner snickered, and thankfully Timothy smiled as well.

"She wasn't my type," Timothy quipped, and Joiner relaxed a little, thinking things were going to be okay. "I know you won't hurt me."

"Then what bothers you? What is it you're most afraid of?" Joiner coaxed and waited long enough that he wasn't sure Timothy would answer.

"What if we're making love and it's not you, but him?" Timothy said with a shudder, and Joiner saw Timothy clamp his eyes closed. "I know he's not here, but...." Timothy shuddered in Joiner's arms.

"Open your eyes, sweetheart. Believe what you see and feel is real, because it is. What's in your head right now is the illusion." Timothy opened his eyes, and Joiner placed his hand over Timothy's heart. "Listen to this; it will never steer you wrong." Joiner tapped lightly, and Timothy nodded. "Will you trust me?"

"Yes," Timothy answered, and Joiner stood up, leading Timothy into the bathroom. One of the things he'd loved when he found this apartment was the huge bathroom. "What's this?"

Joiner turned on the shower and then closed the curtain. "I thought we could try a different venue," he explained. "Will you take a shower with me?" Timothy's eyes widened, and the idea seemed to appeal to him, because he nodded vigorously. "Let me undress you." Joiner opened the buttons on Timothy's shirt, sliding the fabric over his shoulders. "Why are you blushing?"

"Because you keep looking at me like that," Timothy answered, "like I'm special."

"You are special," Joiner countered, stroking Timothy's chest and stomach. "There's nothing broken or wrong with you at all." Joiner sat down, lightly tugging Timothy to him, kissing his chest and stomach, inhaling the intoxicating scent of his lover. He could feel Timothy trembling, but when he looked into his eyes, he saw them sparkling and happy instead of fearful. Opening Timothy's belt and pants, Joiner slid down the zipper and let the jeans slide down Timothy's legs. "Is this okay?" Timothy nodded again, and Joiner slipped down Timothy's briefs, and as he watched, Timothy blushed again. "There's certainly nothing here to blush over," Joiner said as he stroked along Timothy's half-hard length. "You're a handsome man, Timothy."

Joiner pulled off his own shirt and stood up so he could get his own shoes and pants off. Timothy watched but didn't move to him. Once Joiner was naked as well, he reached into the shower and adjusted the water. Turning back, he saw Timothy looking at him, taking him in, but Timothy turned away when he saw Joiner looking back at him. "It's okay to look all you want. It's allowed." Walking to him, Joiner took Timothy's hand, placing it on his chest. "So is touching. There's nothing to be ashamed of."

"I know that. It's just that you're so handsome, and I'm so...." Timothy looked down at himself and turned away. "Pale and skinny."

"You're amazingly attractive," Joiner told him. "See what you do to me," he said, his eyes boring into Timothy's as he approached him carefully. "Just relax and let me make you feel good, okay? Don't worry about anything, and promise you'll tell me if there's something you don't like."

Timothy promised, and they stepped under the water. Joiner maneuvered Timothy directly under the spray, picking up the bar of soap and running it over Timothy's skin. "Feels good," Timothy said softly, and Joiner saw his eyes close but felt none of the tightness and tension Timothy had experienced earlier.

"I know. You need to be touched and cared for. You deserve it," Joiner crooned as he washed Timothy's smooth skin. The man felt like a dream, and he moved wherever Joiner touched him, like everything was brand new, and it probably was. Timothy had told him he hadn't been hugged or had anyone say they loved him in years, and not being touched would go along with that. Joiner washed Timothy's chest and stomach before squatting down to wash his legs. He felt Timothy quiver and heard him hiss softly as Joiner washed his calves and inner thighs. By the time he was done, Timothy was erect, and Joiner soaped his hands good before gripping Timothy's cock, stroking and washing at the same time.

Joiner thought Timothy was going to come unglued. He held his breath and his entire body shook. Joiner's first instinct was to stop, but Timothy placed his hand on Joiner's, and he felt Timothy begin to thrust. Joiner tightened his grip and let Timothy move. Small moans filled the shower, mingling with the sound of the water. When Joiner pulled his hand away, Timothy groaned loudly. "Just stand still," Joiner said as the water sluiced down Timothy's body, washing away the soap. Joiner made sure his hands were soap-free as well before leaning forward, taking Timothy's cock deep into his mouth.

"Holy fuck!" Timothy cried, and Joiner smiled around Timothy's large cock, licking and sucking as he listened to Timothy's cries. He'd already found out that Timothy really liked this, so he stroked Timothy's legs as he ran his tongue around Timothy's cock. The water poured over him, and he felt Timothy's hands on his head. Timothy began flexing his hips again, and Joiner moved with him, encouraging him to take what he wanted. "God, Joiner," Timothy cried as Joiner bobbed his head. Timothy's rich flavor burst on his tongue again and again. Timothy moved in the shower until his back was against the wall, and his thrusting became more urgent, his rhythm ragged. Judging from Timothy's urgent cries, he wasn't going to last much longer. "Joiner, I'm gonna come."

Joiner sucked harder, taking Timothy as deep as he could, and he felt Timothy throb and come deep down his throat. Joiner swallowed and closed his eyes, concentrating on taking what Timothy had to give as his own release raced through him. Joiner felt Timothy slide from between his lips as he stroked himself, and with a deep moan, Joiner came, shaking and crying out the entire time.

As he came back to himself, Joiner noticed a couple of things: the water was beginning to go cold, and Timothy was lightly petting his head. Joiner turned off the water and managed to get to his feet. Timothy immediately hugged him tight, and Joiner felt his lover rubbing his back as Joiner caught his breath.

Timothy began to shiver, so Joiner pushed the curtain aside and grabbed two big fluffy towels. They dried off relatively quickly, and Joiner hung up the towels, leading Timothy to the bedroom, where they crawled under the covers, and Joiner turned out the light. Timothy didn't curl next to him the way he expected, and Joiner rolled onto his side to face him. He waited for Timothy to say something, wondering what was wrong, but Timothy didn't say anything. Eventually, Joiner felt the mattress shift, and Timothy cuddled next to him. Joiner didn't know what Timothy had been wrestling with, but he seemed to have worked through it, and Joiner held his lover until he fell asleep.

CHAPTER 7

"WHAT'S been with you these last few weeks?" Heidi asked from her desk just across the partition from Timothy's. "You've been acting nervous, and even quieter than usual." Timothy heard her stop typing, and when he looked up, he saw her peering at him expectantly. "Boyfriend troubles? Because if it is, I have this friend, he's cute, available, and he would love you."

Timothy shook his head. "No, thanks. It's nothing like that." Timothy had not told anyone other than his supervisor about the whole fighting-the-government thing, and he wasn't interested in telling Heidi. It would be around the office in two seconds. You never told Heidi anything you didn't want the world to know. "I'm just dealing with some stuff from my grandfather's estate, and it's taking a lot of time and effort." That wasn't a lie, and Timothy returned to the drawing he was working on.

"So things are going well with your boyfriend? I'm glad. You're a nice man who deserves someone nice." She smiled at him, and to Timothy's surprise, went back to work, and soon he heard typing and the sounds of work from her desk. Timothy got his mind back on his work just as his phone rang.

"Timothy Besch," he said as he answered.

"It's me." There was a smile in Joiner's voice. "Gerald asked me to call and see if you can meet with us. We have some questions for you, and we need your help." The light tone was gone from Joiner's voice, and Timothy knew he was all business now.

Timothy's nerves ramped up. Gerald and Joiner had called him into the office a few times to update him on the case, but Joiner had never sounded so urgent before. "I can't," Timothy explained. "I'm on a deadline, and I have to get these drawings done today. There's no way I can get to your office in time today."

"Just a minute," Joiner said, and Timothy went back to work while he waited. These designs were critical to the new model, and he had to get them done. He was so close, and his supervisor was waiting on them. She'd been extremely understanding, and Timothy did not want to disappoint her. "Gerald asked if you could come to his house for dinner. We can talk there."

"Okay. Tell him I can be there about seven." Timothy was ready to hang up the phone when he heard something very soft. "What?"

"I said I love you," Joiner repeated, and he then hung up. Timothy smiled and set his phone back in the cradle before returning to his work. He tried desperately to keep focused for the rest of the afternoon, and somehow he managed to finish the drawings and send them to his supervisor before shutting down his computer. Leaving the office, Timothy hurried to his car and drove through town. He parked in front of his own, still largely empty house and walked to Gerald and Dieter's. After ringing the bell, he waited, and Dieter opened the door, immediately pulling him into a hug.

"The confab is in Gerald's office. Let me get you a drink, and then the three of you can talk," Dieter said before hurrying away. He returned with a tray of sodas that he set on Gerald's desk. "Dinner will be ready in an hour. I'm giving you till then to talk business, then I'm calling in the dogs."

Gerald smiled at his partner. "We don't have dogs."

"Actually, I'm going to remedy that. I want a puppy, and I'm thinking of one that will have a special affinity for your shoes," Dieter said, laughing as he left the room.

"He's been talking about getting a dog for months," Gerald said as he popped open a Coke and offered one to the others.

"You work long hours, and he spends a lot of time alone," Timothy said as he watched Gerald. "He needs some company, and maybe some protection, for when you aren't here."

Gerald nodded thoughtfully before turning to Joiner. "We certainly don't want to be late for dinner, so we'll get right to it. One of the things we've built our case around is your grandfather's story. We have all the information from the previous cases, and we can use that, but what this case will hinge on is what makes it different from the others, and that's your story of how your family got the coin."

"I've already told you the story two or three times," Timothy said, feeling frustrated.

"I know, and I'm not asking for a repeat. We've done some research and determined that your grandfather and his dad visited the mint on April 13 or 14, 1933, because on those two days, the temperature in Philadelphia reached almost ninety degrees. The bullion window was still open at the mint, even though they had no need for additional gold since they were no longer pressing gold coins, and at that time there was plenty of confusion surrounding the implementation of the law requiring people to turn in their gold. Unfortunately, the mint's records are not as good as we'd like them to be. However, we can place your family in Philadelphia that month, and Milwaukee in May, so the timing seems right. We can corroborate the story, but we cannot place the coin specifically in that context." Gerald stopped speaking and took a sip of his Coke.

"What we're wondering is," Joiner said, picking up where Gerald left off, "are there any receipts or papers from that time? Have you been through the things in the attic? We can try to make our case with what we have, but it's not likely to sway the judge."

"It's a real long shot, Tim," Gerald said, "and we'll keep working things on our end. But if you could make some time to go through anything that might be around, see what there is. You never know what might help us. Did your grandfather ever write down his story? You telling it becomes hearsay, but if we have it in his own words, that could make a difference."

"I'll look," Timothy said. "There are trunks and lots of boxes in the attic. My mother never went up there, so the stuff is all old. There could be something up there to help, but it's going to take some time to go through."

"Joiner will help you, and so will I. Can we meet at your attic the day after tomorrow?"

"Is this part of the usual legal services?" Timothy asked with a smile he tried to hide behind his soda.

"No. This is what we do for friends," Gerald quipped back.

"Then if you'll help look, I'll arrange dinner," Timothy agreed, and Gerald stood up, carrying the tray from the sodas out of the office. Dieter met them in the hallway. "We're all done, and yes, you can get a dog if you really want one."

Dieter lit up. "Good, because she arrives tomorrow. Her name's Frances, and she's a two-year-old miniature beagle. I'm going to call her Franny, and she can sleep at the foot of our bed." He kissed Gerald and walked happily back to the kitchen.

"Looks like you got played, boss," Joiner said, and Timothy looked around the room, anywhere but at Gerald. Thankfully, Gerald began to chuckle.

"Guess I did. Go on into the living room. We'll be right in," Gerald said, and Timothy wondered if Dieter was in trouble. Waiting in the hall, Timothy heard a squeal followed by laughter he recognized as Dieter's, so he went into the living room and sat next to Joiner. Both Gerald and Dieter joined them in a few minutes, and they talked until a timer went off, then Dieter ushered them into the dining room.

Once the meal was over, Joiner walked Timothy home. "You were quiet most of the evening."

Timothy's thoughts had kept him occupied. "We're going to lose, aren't we?" Timothy stopped walking and looked at Joiner. "Please just tell me the truth."

"We have been. You know what we know. Right now, winning isn't likely, but that can change," Joiner said, and he moved closer to him. Timothy felt the flutter of nervous excitement he'd come to associate with Joiner. He still got nervous about some things, but over the last two weeks they'd explored a lot of things together, and not just in bed. They had really gotten to know one another, and this weekend, Joiner was taking him to meet his mother and stepfather. They were going to go a few weeks ago, but plans had changed. "I'm always truthful with you, and if I can't tell you something, I'm honest about it." Timothy began walking slowly again but remained quiet. "One thing they teach us in law school," Joiner said from beside him, "is never to presume how a jury or judge will rule. Our case isn't as strong as we'd like, and that's why we're looking for more information. That doesn't mean we'll find it, but we have to try. That's as honest as I can be."

Timothy stopped again, this time on the walk to the front door of his house. "Why do you put up with me?"

Joiner chuckled, and that confused Timothy even more. "I don't put up with you, I love you, and there's nothing to put up with. You're you."

"A huge bundle of nervous neuroses," Timothy countered. "We're going to visit your mother this weekend, and I'm scared to death over it. I keep wondering if she's going to like me, and what's going to happen if she doesn't? Then there's sex, and I know you want more than I may ever be able to give, and I worry about this whole government-fight thing, and I...." The words almost tumbled over themselves to get out, and even to Timothy they barely made sense.

Joiner raised his hands in surrender, and Timothy stopped babbling. "First thing, you are not a bundle of neuroses, and it's normal to be nervous when you're involved in a lawsuit. Secondly, if my mother doesn't like you, it's her loss, and we'll turn around and come home. But my mother is going to absolutely love you. Third, as for sex...." Joiner lowered his voice and shrugged. "I've never had a more caring lover."

"But...." Timothy knew there were things he might never be able to separate in his mind.

Joiner touched his arm, and Timothy remembered they were still outside. Opening the door, they stepped into the dark house. "There are no buts... I promised you we'd take things at your speed, and I meant it." Joiner moved closer to him, and Timothy moved into the comforting embrace. "I did want to ask you something, though. I know you have troubles with the thought of anal intercourse, but I was wondering if you'd be willing to...." Timothy heard Joiner swallow. "Would you like to be on the giving end?"

Timothy stilled as memories flooded through him. He felt himself shake as he realized he was standing in nearly the same place where it had happened. "You want me to do that to you?" Timothy felt his breath coming hard and fast.

"It's okay. You're safe, and no one is going to hurt you." Joiner's words cut through his anxiety, and Timothy got his breathing under control. "I promise no one will hurt you." He felt arms around him, and he tried to get away until he realized they were Joiner's. Then he sagged into them, relieved but scared that this was just another example of how totally weird he was. "It's okay, you're fine now." He felt Joiner kiss his hair, and gentle hands soothed away the fear and panic.

"Sorry," Timothy whispered, feeling ashamed.

"You were back there, weren't you?" Joiner asked him.

"For a second, yeah." Timothy felt the shivers abate, and he began to feel much more normal. "Maybe keeping the house isn't such a good idea."

"In all the time you've been here the last few weeks, has it bothered you at all?" Joiner asked, and Timothy thought about it. He realized it hadn't and shook his head. "Then it's not the house, but what I asked you."

"But you want to...," Timothy began, "and I may never be able to do that."

Timothy felt Joiner shrug. "You're a lot more important than something as small as that. When you're ready, it will be there, and until then, there are lots of other things we can do to show our love." Joiner squeezed him slightly. "You already know which of those you like," Joiner added in a deep, sultry voice that made Timothy shudder.

"But I'm such a mess," Timothy whined softly.

"Sweetheart, you had something very traumatic happen to you. The way you feel is understandable, and I was wrong to press you." Joiner moved away, and Timothy missed his warmth immediately. "Let's go. Do you want to go home or come back to my place?" Given a choice, there was no question in his mind where he wanted to be.

They parted, making their ways to their cars, and Timothy met Joiner at his apartment. They went straight to Joiner's room, though Timothy wasn't sure he was in the mood to do anything. But as soon as Joiner climbed into bed with him, Timothy wanted to erase all the remembered pain, and Joiner seemed to do that with ease. It wasn't long before Joiner had him forgetting his name as he cried out so loudly that afterward, he'd worried the roommate had heard him.

IN THE morning, Timothy and Joiner showered together, which was becoming a ritual that Timothy enjoyed immensely. It wasn't necessarily sex, but intimacy and closeness brought from mutual touching and what Timothy knew was love, even if he couldn't yet bring himself to actually say it.

They both left for work, and Timothy spent most of the next two days trying to keep his mind on his work and trying not to mess anything up. He took pride in always doing the best job he could, but he kept finding mistakes that were driving him crazy. Every time he let his mind wander, it would skip from what he was doing to thoughts of Joiner or where they could possibly look for things in the attic. "You can tell me to butt out if you want," Heidi said from across the wall, "but something is bothering you." She signaled him to come over, and Timothy stood up, walking to her work area. "You never make mistakes like this." She pointed to her monitor to where Timothy had put in the wrong specification for the steel. They often checked each other's work, but that was such a newbie mistake. Going back to his desk, Timothy rechecked everything he'd done, finding other small errors and correcting them.

By the end of the second day, Timothy was a nervous wreck and grateful to leave the office. On the way, he picked up sandwiches and some other food before stopping at his apartment for a change of clothes and then hurrying to his house. Joiner was already waiting there, and Timothy let him in. Gerald and Dieter arrived a few minutes later, and after a quick dinner, the four of them headed up to the attic. "I already brought down the things I was going to use," Timothy explained as he pushed open the door into the space beneath the rafters. "What do you think is best?" he asked Gerald.

"Start with the oldest things, go through them in an orderly fashion, and look at everything, especially papers and any notebooks or diaries. If you find something, pass it to me, and I'll look at it further. Joiner and I will take anything with possibilities back to the office. However, make sure someone else sees where you find anything. We could need corroboration."

Timothy moved to the back of the attic and began pulling out some of the old trunks. He set one by Joiner and then returned for more. He also pulled out some boxes that look like they held old papers and records. The others began sorting as Timothy continued opening and looking through everything. In some boxes, he found things he wanted and set them aside before continuing his search. There were at least half a dozen old trunks and wooden boxes along with other things that had been stored up here over the years. The place looked like something out of a Hollywood movie set.

"There's only old clothes and books in this one," Joiner said. "Put it aside, because some of the books looked interesting and you should probably go through them."

Timothy set the trunk with the pile of boxes he needed to look through later and brought Joiner a particularly heavy trunk. Dieter finished looking though his box, and Timothy brought him another before grabbing the last trunk. Hauling it to a free area of floor, he opened it. The trunk was filled with what looked like various-sized smaller boxes, all neatly packed and arranged. Pulling out the first one, Timothy opened it and saw it was full of old black-and-white photographs. Timothy wanted to look through it, but set the box aside and opened the next one, finding more pictures. Box after neatly arranged box filled with pictures came out of the trunk. Toward the bottom, he found cigar boxes lining the bottom, each inscribed with what looked like a year. "Gerald," Timothy called as he lifted out the one marked 1933.

He wasn't sure why he was so excited—there could be anything in that box, and it wasn't as though he could expect the exact piece of paper they needed to be inside with a red ribbon around it. Opening the box, Timothy stared at the contents and gasped. It was filled with bits of stuff. "My God," Timothy gasped. "Grampy used to tell me that when he was a kid, his dad would give him his cigar boxes when he was done with them, and Grampy would put his treasures in them." Timothy picked up what looked like a ring whittled out of wood, rolling it between his fingers. There was a harmonica, tarnished with age, other small bits of paper, and even a pin from what looked like a railroad. "These must be all of them." Timothy set down the one box and opened another as the others went back to work. One of the boxes held an old blue ribbon. Timothy choked up, and after briefly looking in each box, he set them back inside the trunk and placed the other boxes back inside. Closing the lid, he set the trunk aside and began looking for more possibilities.

"Gerald, what about this?" Joiner asked, and Timothy set the box he was carrying on the floor, hurrying to where Joiner held what looked like a journal. "Did your grandfather keep a diary?" Joiner asked him, and Timothy shook his head.

"Not that he ever told me," Timothy answered.

"There are dozens of them in here," Joiner said, pulling out bound books, each inscribed with a year. "I know what these are. They're Daily Aids. My grandmother used to get one at Woolworth's each and every year." Joiner looked through the box. "This one's from 1940." Joiner set the book aside. "And here are 1935 and 1934." Joiner set them both aside and carefully looked through the box again. "And 1933." Joiner pulled out the book and carefully opened the pages. Everyone stopped what they were doing. "The inset says Joseph Harbinger Sr."

"That's Grampy's dad!" Timothy practically jumped with happiness. He wanted to take the book, but he restrained himself as Joiner began carefully turning pages.

"Is there anything for April?" Gerald asked, and Joiner gingerly turned to the proper pages.

"They visited the mint on Thursday, April 13," Joiner said with a smile. "Listen to this: 'The heat was oppressive, and Joey was miserable, but he bucked up like the little man he is. The crush of humanity, however, was more disturbing than the heat, with a few fists being thrown. We waited in line for hours at the hands of bureaucracy and government inefficiency. We waited for hours to turn in our gold coins, only to be given more at the bullion window. In this heat, I was sure Joey would melt clean away, so we stuffed them in our pockets and hurried away from the unbearable crush as quickly as possible.' This is adorable," Joiner said before continuing to read, "'Joey asked as we were leaving if we could get a soda, and one of those sweet concoctions never tasted so good.'"

"Is there anything more about the coins?" Gerald asked, and Joiner continued reading. Timothy felt on pins and needles, barely able to stand still in his excitement. The passage Joiner had read was almost straight out of one of Grampy's stories, and he couldn't wait to read all the diaries. Regardless of what they found out for the case, Timothy felt as though they'd just found buried treasure.

Joiner read silently for a few seconds. "He certainly isn't a fan of government inefficiency. Yes, but he doesn't say anything specific. 'Why the government would press gold coins and turn around and have everyone turn them in is beyond me.'" Joiner handed Gerald the diary, and he seemed happy. "Unfortunately, there isn't much else that's usable. The rest is about his normal life."

"True, but this at least alludes to the fact that he received a coin probably minted in 1933, and then was required to turn that coin right back in. It gives us something to work with. It will at least cast doubt on the fact that none of the coins were ever issued. This is a period account of the confusion that would result if someone were to receive a newly minted coin and then be required to turn it in." Gerald seemed pleased, and he placed the diary in his bag. "Let's see if we can find anything else," Gerald said encouragingly. "Maybe there's more."

There wasn't. They looked through every box and trunk, but there was nothing else that might be helpful. Actually, Timothy thought they'd been quite lucky and was excited. The diary validated a great deal of the story and at least alluded to the coin. He wasn't sure if they were going to win, but some of the fear and doubt he'd experienced the day before seemed to have dissipated. Once everything was packed away again, they all descended the attic stairs.

"We understand you've decided to keep the house," Gerald commented as he and Dieter got ready to go. "Have you planned when you're going to move in?"

"I'll be right back," Dieter said, and he hurried out the door.

"We're visiting Joiner's family this weekend, so I figured the following one. That should give me time to get the last few things done inside," Timothy explained. He was beginning to get excited about the idea, but he wanted everything to be as ready as possible. Not that he had that much to move in, but he was still hoping to get the floors done, and it would be easier with the house empty.

"Say hi to Uncle Timothy, Franny," Dieter said as he stepped back inside, carrying the most adorable little dog. Dieter held her close, and she licked Timothy's cheek. He set her down, and she immediately wound around Timothy's legs before traipsing off to explore the house. "I got her from an animal rescue. They found her running wild in one of the parks, and it took them a month to get her used to people again. But she's adorable and very well trained." Dieter sounded exactly like a proud parent. "Franny," he called, and little toenails clicked on the wood floors as she came running.

"She sticks to Dieter like glue," Gerald said as Dieter picked her up, and they all took turns stroking between her ears.

"Is she getting used to her new home?" Joiner asked when it was his turn to get some doggie loving.

Gerald scoffed lightly. "Are you kidding? She followed Dieter around from the moment we brought her home. If he goes to the bathroom, she whines outside the door. Last night when we went to bed, she whined from her doggie bed on the floor and only stopped when Dieter lifted her onto the bed. That dog is going to be so spoiled. I told Dieter she could sleep in the kitchen on her bed, but no. Now we have a threesome." Gerald didn't really seem too upset, and Dieter glared at him for a few seconds before bursting into a smile.

"I promised we'd put her in the kitchen tonight, but I know she's going to yowl," Dieter warned with the smile of a man who knew he was going to get his own way in the end. "We should head home."

"Thank you for helping," Timothy said to both of them as he escorted them to the door. Closing it behind them, Timothy looked at Joiner. "I could use a drink," Timothy deadpanned, and Joiner grinned.

"How about we couple that with a bit of video game fun?" Joiner was already gathering his things to leave.

"Do you want to clean up first?" Timothy asked. "I have a working shower upstairs."

"Forget video games," he said, taking Timothy by the hand. "Let's play 'get Timothy all naked and wet.' That beats watching a television screen any day." Timothy couldn't argue with that, and he thought the Joiner version of that same game was pretty sweet too.

"But what about the drink?" Timothy asked as they reached the top of the stairs and were nearly at the bathroom.

"I have wine at my place for when we're nice and clean." Never in Timothy's life had he somehow gotten naked so fast.

THANK goodness it was Friday. Timothy had packed a small bag, and he drove right from work to Joiner's apartment. He was nervous as all get-out, but also excited, because Joiner had promised to take him to the museums on Saturday. He'd just pulled up when Joiner hurried out of the apartment. "Are you ready to go?" Timothy popped his trunk, and Joiner transferred the bags to his car.

"Excited much?" Timothy quipped, and he went into the apartment to take care of business. Once he came out, Joiner was waiting for him in the hall. Timothy got a nice kiss and then another. "Okay, now we can leave." Timothy was trying to put the best light on this visit as he could, and trying not to let his own nervousness overshadow Joiner's obvious excitement.

Timothy followed Joiner out to the car and climbed into the passenger seat. "It's going to take a while because of rush-hour traffic, so get comfortable and relax." Joiner pulled out and headed toward the freeway. "How was work?"

"Pretty good," Timothy answered. "I worked on the detailed design for a new bike. They asked for new ideas, so I got permission to design one from the ground up. That's what I've been working on for the last few days. I should have it done soon, and then we'll see if management likes it. How about you?"

"Still working hard. The hearing is late next week. Gerald's still nervous, and we're digging, but unless something new shows up, we're as ready as possible right now."

"Why is Gerald nervous?" Timothy asked with a flutter of nerves in his own stomach.

"He told me he's always nervous, and he always looks for more to back up his case. But we're as confident as we can be, and after we present our case, it will be up to the judge."

"So are you nervous?" Timothy asked.

"God, yes," he answered. Joiner took Timothy's hand, placing it on his leg, and Timothy felt the muscles firing rapidly. "You can be nervous on the inside, but you can't show it on the outside or you're dead." Knowing that Joiner was nervous too made him feel a little bit better. "Have you thought of any other places to look?"

"Not really."

"Did you check where you found the coins?" Joiner asked, and Timothy looked across the seat.

"No. There wasn't anything else up there. At least I don't think there was." Timothy had checked as best he could, but it was pretty dark.

"We can look again when we get back," Joiner said, and Timothy agreed, suddenly wondering if he could have missed something.

Timothy rode in silence for a while, thinking as he nervously chewed a fingernail. "Where are we going? Do they live in Chicago proper?" Timothy pulled his hand away from his mouth, trying to push back his nerves.

"They live in Lake Forest," Joiner explained, "so we won't have to go all the way into Chicago. Carter's office is in the city, but there's a train station on a direct line into the city. It's a really beautiful area." Timothy nodded and stared at the passing scenery. "I know you're nervous, but there's nothing to worry about. Both Carter and Mom are going to like you, and they're both really nice." Joiner took his hand and continued driving. Timothy could not get over how sweet and caring Joiner was.

"So did you spend a lot of time with your mother after she married Carter?" Timothy couldn't remember, and he was trying to keep his thoughts straight.

"Yes. I saw my dad on weekends, but I lived with my mother, and once she married Carter, we moved in with him. Carter very much became like a second father, and as far as I can remember, he never treated us any differently than his own, biological children. We were very lucky in that regard." Joiner turned off the freeway and began heading east toward the lake. As they rode, the area around them shifted from middle-class suburban to more and more expensive areas. The houses got steadily larger, and the lawns sprawled more and more around them. They passed a sign indicating they were in Lake Forest, and started seeing grand homes with wrought-iron fences and massive gates.

"Joiner, do they live in a house like that?" He pointed to a huge white house with a sprawling manicured lawn and huge trees.

Joiner chuckled. "No," he said as he turned off the main road and began winding down shaded side streets with immaculately impressive homes. As the car slowed, Joiner signaled and turned. Timothy gasped as they passed between massive pink-brick gateposts decorated with lions and pulled into the huge circular driveway of what looked almost like a European castle. "I'm sorry, I just couldn't resist."

Timothy stared with his mouth open. "Is this really where your mother lives?"

"In the summer. During the winter, they have a home in Palm Beach," Joiner explained. Timothy heard the engine shut off, and Joiner opened his door. Timothy continued staring and watched as the front door opened and a man stepped out and walked toward the car.

"Mills, it's good to see you," Joiner said as the man approached. Timothy got out of the car, waiting to see what would happen. "This is Timothy Besch."

"Welcome to both of you," Mills said rather formally. "I have your rooms set up and ready. I'll take your bags up." Joiner popped the trunk, and Mills lifted out their bags. "Your mother is on the lanai," he explained.

"Thank you," Joiner said to Mills, and they headed toward the house.

"Thank you for taking care of the bags," Timothy said to Mills and he followed Joiner inside. The house was just as impressive inside as it was outside. The entrance hall soared up two floors, with a grand staircase and a crystal chandelier that must have weighed a ton. Timothy's eyes didn't know where to settle as they moved through the house. At the back of the house, they passed outside, and Timothy found himself under a huge portico decorated as an outdoor living room with tables, wicker chairs, and tall tropical plants.

"Joiner," a slender, elegant woman said as she put down her book and stood up. She hurried to him, hugging Joiner tightly. "I've missed you so." After the formality of the house, Timothy realized he had expected a cooler, more somber greeting.

"Mom, this is Timothy Besch," Joiner said, introducing him. "Timothy this is my mother, Sharon Groves."

"I'm pleased to meet you, Mrs. Groves." Timothy held out his hand.

"Please, call me Sharon, and it's wonderful to finally meet you." She shook his hand. "Joiner has told me so much about you. Please sit down." She motioned toward the chairs. "Carter should be home soon, and I've asked Mavis to serve dinner out here." Sharon sat back down, and then both Joiner and Timothy sat. He felt so out of place in these surroundings. Timothy found himself constantly looking to Joiner to make sure he didn't do anything wrong.

A woman came out pushing a cart. "Thank you," Joiner said, and the woman nodded and left. "What would everyone like to drink?" Joiner stood up and walked to the cart, looking expectantly at his mother.

"A martini would be fine, thank you," Sharon answered and turned to Timothy. "Please don't let this place intimidate you. Around here, we're just like anyone else." Somehow Timothy doubted that as he looked out over the expansive back lawn with its tennis court and huge swimming pool. Finishing the mixing ritual, Joiner handed his mother a cocktail glass. Timothy asked for a white wine, and Joiner poured two glasses before sitting back down. "Carter's family built this place, and his mother was as pretentious as they come. We actually live in a small number of the rooms. I never realized how big this old barn was until all the children moved out and it was just Carter and I. Now there's more staff to take care of it than anything else." Sharon sipped from her glass, and Timothy heard footsteps coming from inside. Turning around, he saw an older man of average height sauntering in their direction.

"Carter," Sharon said pleasantly as he stepped onto the lanai. She seemed genuinely happy to see him. "Joiner's here, and this is Timothy."

"Pleased to meet you, sir," Timothy said after standing up, and they shook hands. Carter's grip was firm and sure.

"It's good to meet you," Carter said, and after releasing Timothy's hand, he pulled Joiner into a brief hug, greeting his stepson before fixing himself a drink.

"So when are you going to let me get you a job at one of the major firms in Chicago?" Carter asked Joiner as he sat in the chair next to Sharon's.

"How about never," Joiner retorted with a smile. "I want to do this on my own." Timothy saw Carter smile with pride behind his glass. "Chicago doesn't have a monopoly on interesting cases. I can't go into details, but right now I'm working on a case against the US Government. Gerald is the lead attorney, but he's had me running point for him, and I've been learning a lot. Besides, you'd have to look pretty hard to find better attorneys than Gerald and Brian, even in Chicago."

Timothy saw Carter's smile widen, and he knew Carter was proud of Joiner, as he should be. Timothy had found in the relatively short time they'd been together that Joiner was a very special man. As

Timothy watched, Carter's gaze moved to him. "What do you do, Timothy?"

"I'm a design engineer," Timothy answered before sipping from his glass.

"He works at Harley Davidson, and right now he's designing a new motorcycle for them," Joiner said. "He's very modest when it comes to most things."

"So how did you meet Joiner?" Carter asked, and Timothy saw that both he and Sharon seemed interested.

"The case Joiner talked about is mine. I met Joiner at his law firm and then again outside the office," Timothy explained.

"Isn't that a conflict of interest?" Carter inquired without malice.

"Only if we tried to hide the relationship, which we haven't, and Gerald is really Timothy's attorney. In fact, Timothy has known Gerald's partner, Dieter, since they were kids. And he's going to be one of their neighbors soon." It was truly a small world sometimes.

The woman who'd brought the cart came out and said something softly to Sharon before turning and going right back inside. "Dinner will be ready soon, so if you need to wash up, feel free," Sharon said, and Joiner set his glass on the table and stood up, so Timothy did the same, following him inside. Joiner led him through the house and up the staircase to the upper floor.

"My room is right here," Joiner said, pushing open the door to a huge bedroom. Timothy peered inside the bright room and then followed Joiner down the hall, where he opened the door to the next room. "You're in here," Joiner told him, and Timothy looked inside at the palatial room with dark, rich colors and masculine furniture. "That door leads to the balcony, and your bathroom is here," Joiner said as he pushed open the door.

"What's that door?" Timothy asked, and Joiner pushed it open.

"That leads to the adjoining sitting room that we share."

Jesus Christ. Timothy had never seen such luxury and space before. His own apartment was small, and these three rooms were almost as large as the entire first floor of his house. "You grew up here?" The intimidation factor was definitely catching up with him.

"It's just a house, Timothy, nothing more. Sure, it's big, but it's just a house. Mom and Carter are just people."

"You could have told me," Timothy said as he followed Joiner into the sitting room and then into his bedroom.

"Yes, I could have," Joiner said before stopping. "But I wanted you to like me for me. Living here does have its price. Lots of people wanted to be my friend growing up simply because of who I was and what they thought I had. This house is really Carter's, not mine, as is the money. He hasn't given me any, other than the help with college, and I don't have some huge trust fund. I wanted you to like me for me," Joiner said seriously before smiling. "Besides, the look on your face when we pulled into the drive was priceless." Joiner hurried around the bed, and Timothy chased after him.

"You little shit," Timothy said happily, and he tossed one of the bed pillows at his lover.

"Come on. If you had known, would it have made a difference, other than making you more nervous?"

"I still would have come with you," Timothy said. He wasn't about to answer the "would it make a difference" part, because he didn't know, but he doubted it. And there was no way he was going to dignify the "more nervous" crack, even if it was probably true. "I'm going to clean up," Timothy said, turning toward the door. "Do we need evening coats for dinner?" Timothy shut the door and heard a pillow thwump into the back side of it. "I'll take that as a no," he quipped through a crack in the door before hurrying to his room.

Timothy opened his small bag and looked at the clothes he'd brought with him. He didn't have anything to wear that didn't make him look and feel like a country cousin. Giving up, he went into the bathroom to wash up—at least he could be clean. When he came back out, Timothy saw a new pair of light dress slacks and a shimmering red silk shirt lying on the bed. Timothy looked toward the door to the connecting sitting room, seeing it open slowly. "I bought those for you," Joiner explained as he cautiously walked into the room. "I know this is a bit overwhelming, and I wanted you to feel welcome."

"You didn't have to," Timothy said even as he fingered the soft fabric. There was no way he could afford clothes like this on his own.

"Hey, I know you were nervous, and you'll look really nice in those. Remember, I know what it feels like to suddenly find yourself plunked down here, when you spend most of your time in the real world. It can be unsettling, and I want you to feel comfortable here. So you can wear the clothes if you like. You don't have to, because I'm just happy you're here with me." Joiner kissed him sweetly before lightly cupping his cheeks and deepening the kiss. The worries that had plagued him seemed to slip away, lost in the taste of Joiner's lips. "I just want you to feel good." Joiner returned to his kisses, and Timothy's mind floated on the passion he felt just below the surface.

A soft knock on the door forced them apart, and then the door cracked open. "Dinner will be served in five minutes."

"Thank you, Mills," Joiner said, and the door closed again. "I'll see you downstairs." Joiner kissed him again and then returned to his room. Timothy looked at the new clothes, and they felt so wonderful that he quickly slipped out of what he was wearing and pulled on the pants. The shirt felt like he was wearing the softest, lightest fabric on earth. Sitting on the edge of the bed, Timothy pulled on his shoes before threading on his dark belt. Checking himself in a mirror, he allowed a smile before hurrying into the bathroom to comb his hair. Then he left the bedroom, walking downstairs and back the way he and Joiner had come.

Timothy stepped out into the evening air, and Joiner turned from where he was speaking to his mother. The smile that lit his face told Timothy he'd made the right choice in deciding to wear the new clothes. Joiner set down his glass and walked to him. "You look good enough to eat," Joiner whispered before escorting him to a table set with fresh flowers and candles.

"Please," Sharon said as she motioned toward a chair, and Timothy pulled it out and took his seat as the others sat as well. Mills came out carrying a tray and placed a small plate of what looked like miniature quiches in front of each of them. "I know it seems rather stuffy, but Mavis loves to cook, and with just the two of us, we eat rather plainly, so I told her to go all out in honor of your visit."

"What do you do for fun?" Carter asked, looking at Timothy, and he swallowed before answering, remembering the manners Grammy had taught him.

"Lately, I've been working on the house I inherited from my grandfather. I've gotten the inside pretty much in shape, and the outside is being painted now. In the spring, I'll landscape. Summer is too hard on new plants. I've been doing as much of the work myself as I can."

"It's a modified Queen Anne Victorian with a huge amount of character," Joiner added with a smile.

"I grew up there with Grampy and my mother," Timothy explained before returning to his food, eating slowly.

"Is your mother still alive?" Sharon asked, and Timothy looked to Joiner because he really didn't want to talk about it.

"Timothy doesn't know, Mom." Joiner explained, and Timothy saw a "don't ask" look cross Joiner's face, but Sharon seemed to ignore it.

"That's a shame," she said, and it looked like she was going to ask more, but Joiner interrupted.

"She's like William," he said curtly, and Sharon's eyes widened. Timothy looked to Joiner, wondering what that was about. Carter gasped softly, and Timothy felt extremely uncomfortable. Sharon was the first to regain her composure, and she nodded her understanding.

"So where is this house of yours?" She sounded normal, with just a hint of tightness in her voice.

"It's in Milwaukee, a block off Lake Drive. As I said, I grew up there, and the amazing thing is that a number of the people I grew up with have returned to those homes. My best friend, Dieter, now lives in the house he grew up in with his grandmother, and Tyler is a few doors down from him, living in what was his grandparents' house too." Timothy knew he sounded excited, but having old friends around was part of the reason he'd decided to keep the house.

"Tell Carter about the coins you found if you want, just not that one," Joiner whispered into his ear.

"Okay," Timothy said. "It's a long story, but my grandfather, before he died, gave me a bit of a puzzle that took me a while to figure out. My mother...." Why did everything come back to her? "My mother was... er, is... an addict." Timothy gave up and said it. To his surprise, Sharon reached across the table and patted his hand.

"We understand the disappointment and heartache that can cause," she said, and then she pulled her hand back. Timothy wanted to ask about it but thought better of it.

"My grandfather didn't trust my mother, so he transferred the house to me, and the puzzle I mentioned led to a cache of gold coins." Timothy told them about the place Grampy had built for him to play in and how the coins had been hidden.

Carter's eyes lit up like saucers. "Are you interested in selling any of them?"

"Carter!" Sharon scolded.

Joiner came to the rescue. "Carter has been collecting US gold coins for years and has quite an extensive collection. He's always on the lookout for the few he doesn't have."

"It's okay," Timothy said. "I'd be happy to show them to you sometime. As near as we can tell, they were my great-grandfather's nest egg, and he passed them to Grampy, who passed them to me. Almost all of them are from Philadelphia. I'm really not interested in selling them, but if there's one that you need for your collection, maybe we can work out a trade." The plates were cleared, and Mills served a small salad with wine-poached pear and pecans.

"After dinner, I'll take you into the office and show you my collection," Carter offered with a smile.

"I'd like that, sir," Timothy said, feeling much more at ease.

"Please, call me Carter," he said quietly, and he began to eat his salad. Timothy did the same, telling his hostess how marvelous the food was. The loud clink of a fork made everyone look, and Timothy saw Carter staring at him. "This lawsuit of yours, it wouldn't have anything to do with...."

"Carter," Joiner said lightly. "We cannot discuss it, per our agreements with opposing counsel."

Carter nodded, but he didn't go back to his food. "Timothy, you must promise me you'll let me see it." Timothy was about to ask what he should let him see, but Joiner nudged him under the table, so he returned to his salad, and the conversation shifted to tennis. Both Carter and Sharon were avid players, and it sounded like Joiner was quite good. Timothy hadn't played since high school gym class, but they tried to talk him into a friendly game in the morning anyway.

The main course, beef with béarnaise, followed the salad, and then there was a fruit dessert that made Timothy question if he'd died and gone to heaven. They lingered around the table for drinks until the sun had set and the only light came from the lanterns all around the gardens.

"It's getting late," Sharon explained as she got up.

"I'll be in shortly," Carter said to Sharon, and then he stood up. Timothy did as well, and he and Joiner followed Carter through the house to what appeared to be Carter's office. The room was the epitome of masculinity, with dark wood-paneled walls, a massive antique desk, and leather chairs that felt as soft as a glove when Timothy sat back into one. Paintings of horses and hunt scenes filled the massive wall panels. One wall was lined with bookcases, and when Carter tugged on one of the shelves, the case noiselessly slid forward and then opened. Behind it was a large safe, and Timothy looked away as Carter worked the dial. He then placed his thumb on a pad, a light flashed green, and then he opened the safe. Inside were drawers, and Timothy watched as Carter opened one and pulled out what looked like a large case. "There is one Gold Double Eagle from each mint and year where they were made, from 1907 to 1932," Carter explained as he opened the lined book, and coin after coin glinted up in the light. "Some of these are extremely rare." Timothy noticed that there was one and only one empty space in the case, labeled 1933.

"I found a number of these along with five-, ten-, and one-dollar coins," Timothy explained as he looked at the coins, his eye traveling back to the empty place.

"Believe it or not, the one-dollar coins are often more valuable that the fives and tens because of the rarity," Carter explained and brought out another book, this one containing one-dollar coins. "They didn't make them for very long, and the mints switched to silver for the singles."

"They're quite beautiful," Timothy said as he looked at them, recognizing that he had some that looked similar, but Timothy could not remember all the years of his coins. He wished he'd brought his list with him.

Carter showed them the five- and ten-dollar coins as well before packing everything away, closing the safe, and sliding the bookcase back into position. Then Carter said good night, and they left the office. The sound of Carter's footsteps faded as he got farther away, and as they walked through the house, Joiner stopped and opened a door to one of the rooms, turning on the lights. Timothy's breath caught as he stepped into the elegant high-ceilinged room with long windows and curtains that seemed to go on forever. A grand piano stood in one corner, covered with framed pictures and furniture that looked so delicate it almost seemed to float above the floor. "This is Mother's favorite room," Joiner said, and Timothy stared from the doorway before venturing inside and wandering slowly around the perimeter. The room felt surprisingly warm and inviting, even though Timothy was scared to sit on any of the furniture. In short, the room was the definition of elegant beauty to Timothy.

"Who are they?" Timothy asked as he looked at the pictures on the piano.

"Do you recognize him?" Joiner said pointing to one of the silver frames. "That's me, when I graduated from Harvard." Joiner set the frame back in its place and handed another one to Timothy. "This is Mom and Carter at their wedding."

"They look wonderful together." They still did, as far as Timothy could see.

"Some people thought my mother married Carter for his money, but they always loved each other," Joiner said, and Timothy handed him back the picture.

"I've been thinking that you should ask if Carter would like to come to the hearing. He's an expert on US gold coins," Timothy said.

"And he'd die to see it." Joiner moved closer, and Timothy felt the heat inside rise very quickly. "Why don't you ask him yourself tomorrow, after I check with Brian." Joiner hugged him tight, and Timothy rested his head on Joiner's shoulder. He was ready for bed, but definitely not ready to go to sleep. Opening his eyes, it took him a second to realize what he was seeing. Suddenly Timothy couldn't breathe, and he began to shake. That face... he never thought he would see it again, and it was here in the same place as Joiner's. Grabbing Joiner tightly, he clung to him as his legs began to give out from under him. Timothy's vision began to swim, and then he realized he was falling.

CHAPTER 8

JOINER had no idea what was happening. All he knew was that Timothy was squeezing the air out of him, and then Timothy's weight rested entirely on him. He felt Timothy's weight shift, and then Timothy was falling through his arms. Joiner tried to support him, but he only ended up falling to the floor as well. "Timothy, what happened?" Joiner asked as he stroked his lover's cheek. "Breathe slowly and carefully," he said. At least Timothy's eyes were open. In most rooms of the house, there was a call bell for the servant, a relic of days gone by, in the floor, and in this room, it was under the piano. Joiner pressed the button and held it down. It wasn't used often, but Joiner was grateful when he heard footsteps in the hallway.

"Can I h—" Mills began before rushing into the room. Timothy was already coming around and beginning to sit up.

"Please bring a glass of water and a cool cloth," Joiner instructed, and Mills hurried away.

"I'm okay," Timothy said, but Joiner didn't believe him. "I just got a shock, that's all." Joiner helped Timothy into a chair, and Mills returned, carrying a tray with water and a cloth. Joiner handed Timothy the water, and he drank a few sips.

"Take it easy," Joiner said, and he took the cool cloth and lightly wiped Timothy's brow. More footsteps sounded in the hallway outside, and Joiner wasn't surprised when Carter and his mother hurried into the room.

"What happened?" his mother asked.

"I'm not sure, Mom," Joiner said. He turned to Timothy, who looked even paler now than he had when he'd first sat up. "He'll be fine." Timothy got to his feet, looking a bit unsteady. Joiner heard him take a deep breath and another sip of water.

"Are you sure?" Joiner could hear the concern in his mother's voice and see it written on her face.

"Yes. Thank you," Timothy answered. "I'm sorry for being a bother." His color was coming back.

"Just sit down for a few minutes," Sharon instructed, and Timothy found a chair and lowered himself into it. Joiner noticed that his mother sat in the next chair. "What happened?" Timothy looked toward the piano, and Joiner saw him wince. The others couldn't have missed it, either.

Sharon reached to the piano and pulled out a picture. How she knew which one Timothy had been looking at was a mystery, and Joiner chalked it up to motherly intuition. "Is this who startled you?" she asked, and Timothy nodded. Joiner saw her show the picture to Carter, who took a step back. Then she showed it to Joiner, and he felt a zing of dread shoot up his spine.

"Mom, Carter, can we talk about this in the morning? I think Timothy has had enough for now." He could tell they were curious, and Sharon set the picture facedown on the piano.

"Of course," she said, and they left the room. Joiner heard their footsteps retreating outside, and he turned to Timothy, still concerned.

"Let's go up to my room, and we can talk," Joiner said, and Timothy nodded blankly. He got to his feet, and Joiner walked with him up the stairs, through the bedrooms they were using, and into the adjoining sitting room. "Can you tell me what happened?" Joiner asked once they were seated.

"Who was that man in the picture? Is he here in the house?" Timothy looked toward the door, and Joiner stood up and shut both of them. The man was shaking again.

"That's Carter's son, William. He and I were never very close, and he left the house a few years after Mom married Carter. As far as I know, they haven't seen or heard from him in years, and I doubt he would be welcome in the house. Why?" Joiner held Timothy's hand. "Does this have something to do with what happened to you?" The realization of what might have happened hit him in the chest as Timothy nodded slowly. "I'll fucking kill him!" Joiner spat, and Timothy flinched.

"But he's your brother," Timothy said, pulling his hand away.

"No, he's not. He's Carter's son from his first wife, and she spoiled William and his sister rotten, the bitch. She reminds me of Mildred Pierce, because she was always blind to what her children did. He was kicked out of the house years ago because of his drug habit and the fact that he showed no interest in getting any help. I know Carter tried, but he wasn't willing." Joiner felt sick that William had been the person who'd hurt his Timothy.

"You believe me?" Timothy asked in a small voice.

"Of course I believe you, and so will Mom and Carter. William has been a disappointment and a source of sadness and regret for years," Joiner added before taking Timothy's hand again. "There's nothing to be afraid of, and I'm not leaving you alone." Joiner led Timothy into his bedroom and closed all the doors. After undressing, Timothy climbed into the huge bed, and Joiner did the same. "The security system has been activated, and there are guards outside the gate and patrolling the street, so there's nothing to worry about," Joiner told Timothy in the darkness as he felt his lover clinging to him. "You're safe, and I won't let anything happen to you." He felt Timothy nod against his chest, but Joiner didn't expect either of them would be getting much sleep.

JOINER felt a kick to his shin and rolled over, stroking Timothy's back as he flailed on the bed. He'd already kicked off the covers and appeared to be running in his sleep. "You're okay," Joiner crooned to a still-asleep Timothy, hoping he would settle down. But instead, he jumped off the bed and stood staring back at Joiner as though he didn't know where he was. "It's okay," Joiner said, and Timothy slowly crawled back into the bed. "You were just dreaming."

Timothy was breathing as heavily as if he'd run a marathon. "I haven't had any like that in a long time," Timothy admitted in the dimness. "I thought they were behind me."

"Seeing that picture must have awakened the fear, but he's gone, and he's not going to hurt you." Joiner rubbed Timothy's back to try to get him to relax, but Timothy was having none of it. So Joiner got up and began pulling on his pants. "Put on some pants and come with me." Timothy nodded, and Joiner guided Timothy to his bedroom, where he slipped into the pants he'd worn when he first arrived. "All the windows are alarmed, and don't enter any of the rooms off the main hall. There are sensors in some of those rooms." Joiner led Timothy back through the house to the kitchen. After punching a code into the panel near the door, he opened it, and they stepped outside into the backyard.

"Why are we out here?" Timothy sounded a little scared.

"Do you see over there on that wall post? There are cameras every third one. This place is like a fortress. Carter got threats some years ago, and he added more security than Fort Knox." A growl sounded behind him, and Timothy jumped, but Joiner held out his hand. "Platz!" he commanded, and the dog came forward and sniffed his hand before sitting down, watching both of them warily.

"Guard dogs?"

"Yes. That's Heinrich. You have to know his commands, and he'd better smell someone familiar." Joiner patted him on the head a few times, and the dog began to pant before trotting off as Joiner led Timothy toward the pool.

"Why out here?"

"It's quiet and there are stars and we're surrounded by security, so no one is going to come anywhere near us," Joiner said as he dipped his hand into the warm water. Without saying anything, Joiner slipped off his pants and shoes before lowering himself into the water. Watching Timothy, he held out his hand and saw him slowly begin to shed his clothes. Then he slipped into the water, and Joiner pulled him close. "We're safer here than anywhere else I can think of," Joiner said as the house loomed over them.

"Can't they see us on the cameras?" Timothy whispered.

"No. Inside, it's the dogs and alarms. The cameras concentrate on the perimeter, so it's just the two of us," Joiner pressed his body to Timothy's. Timothy might have been full of questions, but his body certainly didn't feel insecure or afraid, not in the least. Joiner parted Timothy's legs with one of his, bringing their hips together, and Timothy made a deep, groaning moan as their cocks slid along each other.

"Why does the water feel so soft?"

"It's salt water," Joiner answered before kissing Timothy hard as he moved them to deeper water. The water seemed to glide around their bodies, cocooning them in warmth that matched their skin. Joiner held Timothy in his arms, his lover's legs wrapping around him. "You feel so good," Joiner murmured, and Timothy hummed his agreement. Joiner felt painfully hard, and he could feel Timothy rolling his hips lightly against him. Joiner moved them toward the wide steps and set Timothy on the top one, barely in the water. Joiner pressed Timothy back and rolled his tongue around the head of his cock. Timothy gave a small cry, and Joiner took more of him in his mouth, Timothy's familiar flavor bursting on his tongue.

"God, Joiner," Timothy whispered urgently, listing his body and thrusting forward. Joiner sucked harder, pulling Timothy inside him, listening to his almost strangled cries of delight as Joiner bobbed his head. He knew he was driving Timothy crazy, especially out here in the night. There was something about making love outside that really made Joiner's heart race, and he poured all that energy into making Timothy forget everything that had happened. "Please stop," Timothy whispered, and Joiner's head stilled as Timothy slipped from between his legs. Timothy jumped out of the water, and Joiner wondered what was wrong until Timothy came back with a cushion that he set near the water. Joiner lay on his back, and Timothy straddled him, lowering his cock into his mouth, and Joiner felt wet searing heat surround him at the same time.

In the past few weeks, Timothy had discovered this position, and nothing felt as good to Joiner as being sucked by Timothy with his thick shaft filling his throat at the same time. He felt Timothy thrust lightly, and Joiner stroked Timothy's inner thighs, encouraging him to take what he wanted. It was remarkable how quickly Joiner felt his release come over him, and he sucked harder as Timothy's movements became ragged. Their soft moans intensified, and Timothy throbbed inside him, with his own climax following right behind.

Timothy turned around, his body on top of Joiner's, and they kissed languidly to the sounds of the night. Joiner lightly stroked Timothy's skin as they lay quietly together. "I think I'm tired now," Timothy said softly. They got to their feet and pulled on their pants before walking slowly across the yard. Heinrich checked them out again before curling into a ball on the back patio, and they stepped inside. Joiner led them upstairs, and they stripped down, dried off, and fell into bed. This time Timothy didn't move for the rest of the night.

IN THE morning, Joiner woke to Timothy snoring lightly into his ear. Joiner shifted, and Timothy rolled away. Knowing he wasn't going to get any more sleep, Joiner carefully got out of bed and dressed in the bathroom. Timothy was still sound asleep when Joiner leaned over the bed and lightly kissed his cheek before leaving the room and heading downstairs. He found his mother and Carter sitting on the lanai, with breakfast on the table. "How is he?" his mother asked as Joiner sat down.

"He's okay. Shaken up, but he'll be okay, I think," Joiner answered. "He's still asleep, and hopefully he'll be that way for a while."

"Do you know what about William scared him?" Sharon asked as she poured herself a glass of juice.

"I do. You know that Timothy's mother was an addict, and it seems that her supplier was William, at least for a time. Once, in exchange for a fix she needed, she gave Timothy to William, and he...." Joiner looked out across the yard. "I can't say it." Joiner heard a glass shatter, and he saw that Carter had turned completely white. "He doesn't blame any of us, but when he saw the face of the man who...." Joiner clamped his eyes closed. "He wasn't expecting it, and I think he got overwhelmed, then he was afraid William was in the house." This was so screwed up.

"William did that?" Carter asked under his breath, like he couldn't believe it. "My own flesh and blood."

"Yes, he did, without a doubt. But you aren't responsible for him any more than Mom or I are. I know you feel that way, but he made his own choices, and he's hurt a lot of people. You did the best you could for him, just like you did your best for all of us." Carter looked miserable, and Joiner felt he had to reassure him. Carter was usually very strong and rather stoic when it came to emotional displays, but this seemed to have broken through that exterior.

One of the housekeepers swept up the glass and brought another one. "Thank you, Emily." She nodded and then left. A few minutes later, Timothy joined them, still not quite awake, but looking okay.

"I'm sorry about last night," Timothy said softly.

"There's nothing to be sorry for," Joiner's mother said, and Joiner saw Timothy look from person to person. When his gaze settled on Joiner, it chilled Joiner to the bone. "We understand what drugs can do to people, and how they can hurt innocent people." The sadness in his mother's voice must have affected Timothy, because his expression softened, and Joiner released the breath he'd been holding.

Timothy's gaze settled on Carter, and Joiner knew he couldn't miss the agonized look on his stepfather's face. "Joiner told you what happened?" Timothy looked embarrassed and uncomfortable.

"He told us only enough so we could understand," Carter explained. "If there's anything we can do to help make this right...."

Timothy shook his head. "It was a while ago, and you aren't responsible." Timothy looked around the table. "None of you is. The sins of the son are not the sins of the father." Timothy continued to look uncomfortable, as did everyone else around the breakfast table, and everyone seemed to sink into their own thoughts. Timothy's phone began to chime a familiar ring tone that told Joiner that Dieter was calling. Timothy excused himself and stepped away from the table as Mills approached. Joiner asked him to bring a plate for Timothy, and it arrived as Timothy returned to the table.

"What did Dieter have to say?" Joiner asked after swallowing a bite of egg.

"He called to check up on me, and mostly he talked about the dog. By the way, Franny's fine." Timothy rolled his eyes, and Joiner was very pleased talking to Dieter seemed to have lifted his spirits. "I talked to Gerald as well," Timothy said as he sat down, and Joiner couldn't have been more pleased that the topic of conversation seemed to be changing. From the looks around the table, everyone else was as well. "Carter, I know it's short notice, but there's a hearing later this week in Milwaukee. If you can make it, there's something there that might be of interest to you. We aren't to talk about it, but I think from our conversation yesterday, you've figured out what we're talking about, and—" Joiner saw Timothy swallow hard.

"Is this one of the pieces you received from your grandfather?" Carter asked, and Timothy told the story as they ate. "It sounds like you have quite a family legacy," Carter added once Timothy was finished.

"Yes, it is, and we found a diary that confirms the story, which was really exciting." The mood around the table had lightened considerably. They continued talking, with Carter trying to bring up politics, and Joiner's mother shooting him "don't go there" looks.

"What do you have planned for today?" Sharon asked once the dishes had been cleared.

"I was going to take Timothy into town so he could look around for a while, and then we're taking the train into the city. Timothy has never been to any of the museums, so I promised I'd take him."

"I'd really like to see the T. rex," Timothy explained. "We talked about the Science and Industry Museum but settled on the Field Museum."

"Will you be back for dinner?"

"We expect to be," Joiner answered as they got up from their chairs, and after saying their goodbyes, they cleaned up quickly before leaving the house.

Timothy had a ball as they wandered around Lake Forest, poking into a few shops. Then they walked to the station and caught the train into the city. They spent part of the time at the museum, where Timothy did indeed get to see Sue, the Field Museum's complete Tyrannosaurus rex. Then they wandered through the city, stopping into what was once Marshall Field's—and always would be to Chicagoans, regardless of the name that was now on the door. They bought Garrett's caramel and cheese popcorn, and even wandered around Buckingham Fountain before taking the train back to Lake Forest. The entire day, Timothy had looked and acted like a kid in a candy store, and when they returned to the house, Joiner's mother explained that she'd given most of the staff the rest of the weekend off, and they were having dinner at their country club. "It's casual," she'd reassured them, and even Carter didn't wear a jacket.

The rest of their weekend was quiet, with plenty of time to visit and no additional shocks or mishaps. By the time they left late Sunday afternoon, Joiner noticed that Timothy seemed much more at ease and less guarded than he had when he arrived. "Carter and your mother were not what I was expecting," Timothy confessed on the drive home. "After I saw the house, I expected—I don't know what I expected—but they were warm and welcoming."

"They loved you too, and said you were welcome to visit anytime you wanted. They also hoped we would be able to visit them this winter in Palm Beach. So I'd say you made quite an impression."

"By nearly fainting on their living room floor?" Timothy said. "I'll say I made an impression."

"It wasn't that, but the way you handled yourself afterwards. Carter has always had unresolved issues where William is concerned. Carter supported him for a long time, but eventually cut him off, and I think he felt guilty about it. You didn't blame him, and I think he expected you to."

"What happened wasn't his fault," Timothy said, and they lapsed into quiet for a while.

The weekend hadn't been what Joiner had been expecting, but even with the surprise about William, they'd had a good time. And his mom and Carter had truly been taken with Timothy, which was wonderful. Now they had to get through the hearing, and hopefully then Timothy would relax. The one thing that bothered Joiner was that Timothy had never said how he felt. He knew Timothy cared for him, and he'd told himself he didn't need to hear the words, but he really did. And he hoped he wasn't deluding himself regarding how he thought Timothy felt. He'd promised to give Timothy time, and he would, but he still longed to hear the words.

CHAPTER 9

TIMOTHY didn't know how he was going to stand it anymore. The hearing was to start tomorrow morning, and he was a nervous wreck. He'd been fine when he and Joiner had visited Joiner's parents, but he hadn't seen Joiner since the morning after they got back, and his nerves were taking over. He didn't worry so much when he was with Joiner, but he certainly was now. After work, he'd decided to try getting some chores done at the house. He'd planned to tackle doing the work on the better of the bathrooms, but all he was managing to do was gouge the walls and his fingers as he tried to remove the old wallpaper. At least he got all of it off the walls. Cleaning up his mess, Timothy wandered around looking for something to do where he couldn't possibly take one of his fingers off. He had never been so grateful for a knock at the door in his life.

Peering out the window, Timothy saw Joiner standing on his front step, and he couldn't get the door open fast enough. Joiner stepped inside, and Timothy was immediately hugged and then kissed hard and deep. Joiner's tongue took charge of his mouth, and Timothy moaned into the onslaught. "I missed you," Joiner said once he ended the kiss, leaving Timothy's head spinning.

"Me too," Timothy agreed, his lips still tingling. "I wasn't expecting you."

"We've done all we can do, so Gerald kicked me out of the office and said I was to come see you."

"I'm glad you did," Timothy said with a smile as he closed the door.

"What did you do?" Joiner asked, taking his hand and examining the cuts. "Did you clean them out?"

"I was working on the bathroom, and a fight broke out between my putty knife and the wallpaper. I lost," Timothy quipped, but he was enjoying the feel of Joiner's hands on his. "And yes, I washed them out well." Timothy moved back into Joiner's arms. "Did you try to call?"

"No. I came right here from the office and was going to go on to your apartment, otherwise, because we never did look at where you found the coins," Joiner told him, and Timothy nodded. They had planned to check after they got back from Chicago, but their minds had been on other things.

"Let me get a flashlight, and we can look. I doubt there's anything there, but you're welcome to look. I poked around in there Monday, but didn't see anything," Timothy explained, as they went into the kitchen. Timothy retrieved the flashlight as Joiner took off his coat and tie, and then he led Joiner up both flights of stairs and into the attic. "Why do you think this will do any good?"

"I have this feeling that your grandfather knew what he had," Joiner said, and Timothy stopped on the attic stairs, turning to face him. "These 1933 Gold Double Eagles have been the things of legend for decades, and the government has been looking for them for almost seven decades. I suspect your grandfather knew what would happen if it was found, and that's part of the reason he hid them," Joiner explained. "And if that's true, then I would hide any documentation that I had with them as additional protection. The coin alone is only that, but with some additional documentation, then you or whoever in your family had to fight for it could do so."

Timothy nodded and resumed climbing the stairs. "Grampy was always pretty sharp." At the top of the stairs, Timothy turned on the light and pulled the boxes away from the hideaway entrance. Opening the toolbox, Timothy pulled out the screwdriver, and after opening the door, he crawled inside, making room for Joiner as well. Timothy removed the cutout panel using the screwdriver and set it aside, handing Joiner the flashlight.

Joiner had rolled up his sleeves, and he took the light, peering inside the opening. Timothy knew what he'd see: the space where the coins had been and then some old insulation. "Would you hand me the screwdriver?" Joiner asked, and Timothy placed it in his hand. "This is probably a waste of time," Joiner said. Timothy saw him poking the screwdriver inside the hole. With a sigh, Joiner handed him back the screwdriver and the flashlight.

"Grampy sure built you a great place to play," Joiner commented, and Timothy began to back out of the room. Once out, he stood up and waited for Joiner, who followed right behind him. Even though he hadn't been expecting to find anything, he still felt disappointed, and he sighed out loud before putting the screwdriver back in the toolbox.

"You're a mess," Timothy said at Joiner's now partially white pants. Joiner began dusting them off, and Timothy looked around. "Where's the flashlight?"

"I must have left it," Joiner said, and he crawled back inside. Timothy heard a few bumps, and then all movement in the wall stopped. "Timothy!" Joiner cried and then backed out of the door. "I heard something move in the wall." Joiner sounded excited, and Timothy felt his heart race, not that he really figured it was anything other than the crap inside the walls of an old house. Timothy brought over the old toolbox, and they found a cutting blade. Joiner took it and climbed back through the small door. Timothy did the same, holding the flashlight as Joiner cut through the plasterboard. "I need something better," Joiner said, and Timothy crawled back out, searching through the toolbox.

He found a small saw and passed it to Joiner. "Does this work?" He wasn't too keen on Joiner cutting into the play area Grampy had made for him, even if he wasn't going to use it again. He heard sawing sounds, and after a few minutes, Joiner called to him, and Timothy ducked inside. Joiner lowered the section of wall and pulled out a thick plastic bag with papers in it that had been resting against the insulation.

Carefully, Joiner removed the envelope, and Timothy took it, backing out. Joiner handed him the tools and flashlight before backing out as well, covered with even more dust and bits of insulation. "What do we do now?"

"We need to get this over to Gerald and tell him where we found it," Joiner said as distant thunder rolled outside.

"Okay," Timothy agreed, even though he was dying to see what was inside, but the hearing was in less than twelve hours. There were no guarantees that anything in there was going to help them, but if it did, they had to get it in Gerald's hands. Leaving everything where it was, Timothy and Joiner headed toward the stairs, turning off the lights and closing the doors.

Joiner was already on the phone. "Gerald, we found something." They descended the main stairs to the hall. "Timothy and I are on our way over. We should be there in just a few minutes." Thunder rolled again, and Timothy pulled open the front door and stopped dead, staring into the face of his worst nightmare.

"Your mother owes me money, and I'm going to take it out of you!" William threatened.

"William, what the fuck are you doing here?" Joiner yelled from behind him. Timothy saw the surprise on the drug dealer's face. Timothy had no idea where it came from or why he did it, but without thinking, Timothy lashed out, kicking hard at his one-time assailant's crotch. All that registered was a crunch, followed by a cry, and then the fucker who had hurt him was rolling on the ground, yelling and screaming. Timothy raced to him, kicking, gouging, and hitting as all the rage and fear, shame, hurt, self-loathing, and downright terror burst out of him. Someone tried to pull him away, and he shook them off before going back at William.

"Timothy!"

He heard a voice snap from outside, and looked up as Joiner pulled him away. Hugging Joiner tight, he felt tears bust out of him like an atomic explosion. "I love you, Joiner. I love you." Everything in his mind was muddled except that one overriding thought, even as his tears continued running down his face. Over time, he heard other people approach, and eventually he realized it was Gerald and Dieter as well as police officers, but Timothy clung to Joiner as other people moved around him, his head buried against Joiner's shoulder.

"Timothy, we need to talk to you," someone said to him, but Timothy paid no attention. He simply clung to Joiner, willing himself not to look. "Sir, please." Lightning flashed and thunder cracked, but Timothy barely noticed it.

Eventually, he backed away and turned to a uniformed police officer.

"Timothy, this is Kenny from the party. He's a friend," Gerald explained.

"He raped me!" Timothy cried as he rushed toward where William was still lying on the ground. "And he's a drug dealer." Timothy's thoughts were all jumbled, and while he thought he was making perfect sense, Joiner would later tell him he'd been barely comprehensible. Joiner took him inside the house, and Gerald went with them. Someone must have gotten a chair from the kitchen, because Joiner sat him down, and the police officer, Kenny, stood off to the side.

Gerald handed him a glass of water, and Timothy drank it, beginning to feel a little more normal. "Timothy, I have to ask you some questions. You said he raped you?" Kenny asked.

"Yes," Timothy answered, and he told Officer Kenny the story, trying to remember everything. "He threatened me tonight, and I just went off. Is he dead?"

"No. The last I saw, he was moaning pretty loudly. We're taking him into custody because we've been trying to get our hands on him for quite a while."

"I heard the threat," Joiner said from next to him, and Timothy took Joiner's hand because he knew Joiner was choosing him over his stepbrother. "You should also know that William is my stepbrother."

Timothy watched as Kenny wrote down everything. "I think that's enough for now," Gerald said in his best lawyerly tone. Timothy looked to Gerald, thanking him silently.

"The papers," Timothy said frantically, looking around.

"It's okay, I have them," Gerald said, "and both Joiner and I will be here until everyone leaves." Timothy nodded and watched out the front door as lightning flashed again, and the sky seemed to open up.

Another officer stood in the doorway. "I bet we find plenty in the car once we've impounded it," he said, and Kenny nodded. They didn't elaborate, but Timothy knew what they meant.

"We're taking him into custody, so you won't have to worry about him any longer. We probably can't charge him with rape, but we'll get him on plenty of other things." Kenny took down some additional information and thanked them all before leaving the house. Then, one by one, the flashing lights outside began to diminish as everyone left.

"Damn, Timothy," Dieter said once he closed the door, "you beat the crap out of him. Way to go!"

Timothy was mortified and wanted to crawl away. "I hurt someone."

"Hey," Joiner said softly. "You lashed out at someone who hurt you badly, and you've lived with that hurt locked away inside you for a long time. So I'm with Dieter on this one." Joiner sounded confident, and Timothy looked at everyone in the room.

"As your lawyer, I have to advise against clobbering everyone that comes to your door, but in this case, I'd say the bastard had it coming, and it was probably about time someone gave it to him." Gerald walked toward the door. "If you need me, call, but I have to see what we have with these papers, and I don't have much time to do it." Gerald touched Dieter's arm before leaving the house at a run.

"You're going to be okay now, Timothy," Dieter said, and Timothy realized it wasn't a question. "You stood up for yourself against the boogieman and you won." Dieter smiled, and Timothy realized he was right. "You are going to be just fine." Dieter leaned down and gave him a hug. "There's no reason to be scared," he whispered in his ear, "because if you can do that, you can do anything." Dieter hugged him one more time and then straightened up. "I'd better get home myself, or Franny won't leave Gerald alone." Dieter walked toward the door and then turned and hurried back, hugging him again. "You were so brave," he whispered into Timothy's ear, and this time Timothy smiled and let himself believe that maybe Dieter was right.

The house seemed quiet now with everyone but Joiner gone, and Timothy closed his eyes, listening to the rain. He used to do that a lot as a child, and it soothed him now just as it did then.

"Dieter's right, you know. You are brave," Joiner said.

Timothy scoffed and shook his head. "That's why I broke down and cried like a baby in your arms."

Joiner took his hand and held it. "I had a friend before I went to law school who was a Marine, and he used to tell me that Marines ran toward the gunfire. That's what you did today, and I've never met a Marine who wasn't brave, so you can tell yourself whatever you want, but Dieter was right. You faced your fear head-on. So the next time you have a nightmare about your attacker, just remember that you kicked his ass."

Timothy smiled, partly because Joiner was right, and partly because of the silly grin on his face. "Okay, I believe you."

"Good," Joiner said, and Timothy felt him press something into his hand. "This is a key to my apartment. Please go there if you want. I have to meet with Gerald and see what we found, but I'll meet you there as soon as I can, I promise." Joiner kissed him hard. "You're the bravest, sexiest man I have ever met, and as soon as I get back to my apartment, I plan to show you just how much in every way I can." Timothy was kissed ravenously, and then Joiner moved away. "Just think about that until I get there."

Timothy nodded and watched as Joiner opened the door to leave before rushing back and kissing him again. "I'll be waiting for you," Timothy said, and Joiner hurried out into the rainy night.

Timothy's mind was spinning. So much had happened in the past few hours that he barely knew where to turn or what to do. Closing up the house, Timothy left and walked to his car. The rain had let up, and he climbed inside and drove toward Joiner's. When he arrived, Timothy popped the trunk and pulled out an umbrella. Instead of going inside, Timothy opened the umbrella and began walking down the sidewalk. The rain started again, but he really didn't care. His spirit felt lighter.

"I did it, Grampy. You always told me I was sweet and kind on the outside, but made of steel on the inside," Timothy said out load as the rain pounded the umbrella above him. "I never believed you, but I guess you were right. Tomorrow is the hearing, and I don't know how long it will take, but I'm going to fight for what you left me. You deserve it, and so do I." Timothy turned around and began walking back toward Joiner's house as the water soaked into his shoes. "This is our legacy: yours, mine, and even your dad's, and I'll fight to keep it." As Timothy approached the front door, he pulled the key Joiner had given him out of his pocket and let himself inside.

Timothy closed the door and turned on a light in the living room. Sitting on the sofa, he turned on the television. It wasn't long before he grabbed one of the pillows, and soon he lay down and the tension and excitement of the evening leeched out of him as Joiner's scent surrounded him from the pillow. He hadn't slept well in days. His eyes closed, and the next thing he knew, a soft voice was rousing him and tender lips brushed his cheek. "I'm sorry I was so long," Joiner said, and Timothy yawned and slowly began to sit up. The television was off, and Timothy got to his feet and blankly followed Joiner through the now dark apartment. In the bathroom, he cleaned up and then climbed into bed. Timothy was half-asleep again when Joiner slid in next to him, and Timothy curled right to his lover. "Did you really mean what you said?" Joiner whispered, and Timothy felt his arm pull him tighter. "It wasn't just what happened, was it?"

"No," Timothy said as he angled his face toward Joiner's. "I love you, and I'll say it every day for as long as you'll have me." Timothy swallowed, and he felt Joiner's weight shift, then he was on his back looking up into Joiner's eyes.

"Is this okay?" Joiner asked, and Timothy kissed him. Things had changed in the past few hours, and he felt lighter without all the fear to weigh him down. He couldn't say he wasn't nervous, but the panic that usually welled up when he was held down didn't happen. Instead, he saw the love in Joiner's eyes, and he let that be his focus. Joiner kicked off the covers, and Timothy felt his lover's eyes rake down him. "You're beautiful, Tim, really beautiful."

Joiner kissed him, but not on the lips. Instead, kisses trailed all over his skin, everywhere. Timothy quickly forgot everything but where Joiner's mouth was going to go next. "Would you roll over for me?" Joiner asked, and Timothy flashed him a wary look but did as he was asked. He trusted Joiner and knew he wouldn't....

"Holy Christ!" Timothy cried as Joiner zeroed right in on his butt. He felt Joiner's tongue and lips licking and sucking on his skin, and then his cheeks were pulled apart and Joiner's tongue did things he never knew were possible. "What's that?" Timothy gasped.

"It's called rimming." Joiner rolled the R, and Timothy felt warm air against his wet skin; he both gasped and throbbed at the same time. Then Joiner's tongue was back, and Timothy stopped thinking. In fact, he stopped everything except moaning and what he was sure was a bit of begging. Joiner made his body feel things that Timothy had never dreamed of, and when Joiner pulled his hips up, he went right along without thinking. All the hang-ups and fears he'd always had about anyone touching him on the butt, let alone allowing himself to possibly get any pleasure from his backside, fell away.

"Do you like that?" Joiner whispered.

"God, yes," Timothy cried, and he felt Joiner kiss his way up his back until he felt nibbles on his neck as Joiner's erection settled between his cheeks.

"Don't worry. I have no intention of going any further," Joiner whispered into his ear and then sucked on it. "But I want you inside me."

Timothy stilled. "Are you sure?" For a second, what happened to him flashed through his mind.

"Trust me. When you make love, it's wonderful. I want to show you that it can be beautiful and loving." Joiner stilled, and all Timothy could hear was his warm voice in his ear. "I want to replace your bad memories with ones we make together." Joiner sucked on his ear again, and Timothy groaned and shifted into the sensation. "I love you, Timothy." Joiner wrapped his arm around him and held their bodies together while he lightly plucked at Timothy's nipples.

"I love you too," Timothy moaned as he arched his back, turning his head so he and Joiner could share a kiss. "I'm not sure what to do," he admitted, and he felt Joiner chuckle before kissing him again.

Joiner had him roll over, and to Timothy's surprise, Joiner straddled him, gently stroking his chest with warm hands, and their eyes met. Joiner reached over to the bedside table. Timothy heard the sound, but his concentration was on Joiner's eyes. A strange sound drew his attention, and then Joiner straightened back up, wrapping his hand around Timothy's cock.

Timothy thrust into Joiner's grip, and he saw Joiner smile. "Wait until you're buried inside me," Joiner crooned softly. "I'm going to grip you even tighter." And Timothy jumped when he did just that. Then the grip was gone, and Timothy saw Joiner reach for the small bottle, slicking his fingers.

"What are you doing?" Timothy asked, because he expected Joiner to touch him again, but instead he saw Joiner's eyes roll back slightly and heard his breath hitch. Then he knew what was happening, and Timothy shivered, wishing he could see Joiner's fingers probing himself. After years of avoiding thinking of anything anal as sexy, this image sort of blew his mind for a few seconds, but he didn't have time to dwell on it as Joiner's weight shifted. After a tearing sound, what he assumed was a condom was rolled down his cock, and then the air whooshed from his lungs as he was indeed surrounded by an intense heat that made his head throb. All he wanted to do was thrust, but something told him to hold off, and Joiner sank further down onto him.

Timothy's cock felt as though it were being squeezed in the most amazing vise ever created. "Fuck, you feel good," Joiner gasped as his butt met Timothy's hips. Timothy had no idea what to think or say. His mind was totally blown, and he wasn't sure what to do. "Do what your body tells you."

Timothy took that advice and began to thrust up into Joiner. "Oh my fucking God!" he cried as Joiner's hot body gripped his cock. He thought Joiner's hand had felt wonderful, but this was fucking amazing. Then Joiner lifted himself off him, and Timothy groaned, wondering what was happening, even as Joiner rested on his back and lifted his legs. Timothy got the idea, positioning himself between Joiner's legs and sinking into his body. If possible, Joiner felt even better now, and when Timothy began to move, Joiner grabbed him behind the neck and pulled him down into a hot sloppy kiss.

"That's it. I want you to fuck me hard and fast. I want you so badly I can't stand it." Joiner arched his back, and Timothy saw Joiner's mouth fall open as Timothy snapped his hips as fast as he could. "I've wanted this since I first met you," Joiner said. "Change the angle a little," he added breathlessly, and when Timothy did, Joiner yelled and gripped him even harder. Timothy thought he might have hurt Joiner, and he stopped moving, watching his lover's face.

"Please don't stop," Joiner said, and he began moving slowly again.

"I don't want to hurt you," Timothy gasped quietly, still worried that he might have done something to Joiner, and he couldn't bear that. Up until the past few minutes, what he was doing he'd always associated with pain and fear.

"You couldn't. As long as you're making love, you'll never hurt me," Joiner reassured him, and Timothy began moving faster.

Timothy's entire body began to zing as his blood coursed through his veins. Leaning forward, Timothy continued moving in quick thrusts as he kissed Joiner's lips, and then began feasting on his lover's neck. Every time he inhaled, Joiner's intense scent filled his nose, and he loved every breath. Everything about Joiner made him happy, and all of his senses were filled with one person, the man he hoped would love him for the rest of his life. His one and only Joiner. "I love you," he kept murmuring over and over, almost without even realizing it. Timothy's heart felt so full he couldn't hold it in, and for once he didn't try.

"I love you too," Joiner told him, and Timothy felt Joiner tighten around his shaft once again. This time Timothy faltered, the pleasure almost too great.

Joiner's eyes bored into him, and for a few seconds, Timothy could almost see inside his lover's mind. Timothy knew it was just an illusion, but he held onto it, because the feeling faded quickly as his climax approached. Joiner was already stroking himself and telling Timothy to fuck him into the middle of next week. He never knew what that meant until he picked up the pace and Joiner screamed and started coming, pulling Timothy into his own amazing climax that never seemed to end.

Timothy could barely see after riding a wave that seemed to go on forever. Joiner's hands on his skin brought him back to the present, and Timothy let himself be drawn down into Joiner's strong arms. "Love you, sweetheart," Joiner said into his ear, and Timothy smiled as Joiner held him tight. Timothy felt himself slip from inside Joiner's body, and he winced at the sensitivity. He didn't want to move an inch, but slowly he got up anyway and walked into the bathroom. After cleaning himself quickly, he returned with a warm cloth that he used to carefully and lovingly wash Joiner's skin, kissing the skin after the cloth passed. Everything seemed richer and warmer now that his fear had slipped away. Joiner took his hand and Timothy gazed into Joiner's smiling eyes with his own unexpected joy.

"I don't deserve you," Timothy said, still smiling, because he knew that Joiner loved him.

"We deserve each other. You said you'd love me for as long as I'd have you." Joiner brought Timothy's hand to his lips. "What if I told you I plan to love you forever, would that be okay? Because I have no intention of ever letting you go."

"Sounds like perfection to me," Timothy replied as he leaned over the bed to kiss Joiner. He squeaked and dropped the cloth when Joiner grabbed him and pulled him onto the bed, laughing deeply before a kiss drove the rest of his words away. Timothy forgot everything other than Joiner and climbed onto the bed, returning the kisses with everything he had. Joiner was his and always would be. Curling next to his lover, Timothy let happiness and contentment settle over him—deep happiness that he'd rarely felt before.

Timothy knew he would never have faced up to his fears without Joiner, and he knew the reason he finally felt free of the fear that had held him back was because of Joiner as well. Since he'd met him, his life had been brighter, happier, and, well... more like living.

Joiner kissed him again before sliding off the bed. Timothy watched as he picked up washcloth he'd dropped before tossing it into the bathroom and turning out the light. Timothy closed his eyes and let the sound of the now gentle rain and Joiner's soft breathing lull him to sleep. Every now and then he'd carefully turn his head just to make sure he wasn't dreaming already. Eventually, he closed his eyes, happy and content. For now, he was able to successfully keep the nerves and jitters at bay regarding the hearing that would start in the morning. There was plenty to worry about then, but for now, he was loved, and that was what mattered. In the morning he'd deal with the rest, but for tonight the world was outside, and only he and Joiner mattered. After giving Joiner a final kiss, Timothy closed his eyes and finally drifted to sleep.

Timothy woke with Joiner next to him. For a few seconds he stared up at the ceiling, until everything from last night barreled into him: William, the police, what he'd done. "It's okay, sweetheart," Joiner said groggily from next to him, tightening an arm around his waist, and pressing his chest to Timothy's back. "It's okay."

Timothy felt himself shaking like he was cold, but he wasn't. "No, it's not. I nearly killed someone, and today is the hearing, and...." Timothy buried his face in the pillow to stop the rambling, realizing he could stop what he was saying, but not the voices in his head.

"One thing at a time," Joiner whispered into his ear. "Stick to one thing at a time. What you did last night was self-defense, nothing more. You were protecting yourself, and me, from someone you thought was a threat." Timothy turned to look at Joiner. "Never feel bad about protecting what belongs to you," Joiner said, kissing Timothy's shoulder and nuzzling his ear. Timothy nodded and did his best to let go of that worry.

"What about the hearing?" Timothy asked softly as he pressed closer to Joiner. Actually, he was trying to burrow underneath him.

"Gerald said that this morning is going to be mostly procedural things. He and the opposing counsel, along with the judge, need to agree to the rules of how the hearing will work. Some things have been set up, but there are things that need to be said and discussed. This will last today and tomorrow, so there's nothing to worry about now."

"When will I need to bring in the coin?"

"That's one of the things Gerald needs to work out." Joiner went quiet, and Timothy did as well, the two of them lying together as dawn began to light the windows. Timothy's stomach was tied in knots, and he felt Joiner shift on the bed. After a kiss, Joiner got up, and Timothy did the same. He wasn't going to sleep anymore, so he cleaned up and got dressed, heading downstairs to Joiner's kitchen. The coffee was ready, and Timothy sat at the small kitchen table silently drinking his coffee. His thoughts swirled through his mind as he shifted from concern to worry and back again. Joiner's phone rang somewhere in the house, and Timothy heard the ringing stop and Joiner speaking to whoever had called, probably Gerald. Timothy continued sipping his coffee as Joiner walked into the kitchen, the phone at his ear. Joiner poured his coffee and sat across from him, still talking on the phone, and Timothy tuned it out. When Joiner hung up, Timothy raised his eyes from the mug in front of him.

"Was that Gerald?"

Timothy nodded from behind his mug. "He said that you won't be needed this morning and you could go to work. We'll call you if something changes, but he said this is going to be really boring to start with." Joiner set down his mug and walked behind him, sliding his hands down Timothy's chest as he leaned close. "There really isn't much you can do right now but try to go about things as normally as possible. I promise I'll call you during the breaks to let you know what happens."

Timothy knew Joiner and Gerald's logic was right, but…. "If you don't need me there…."

Joiner ran his fingers along Timothy's ribs, and he nearly snorted coffee out of his nose. "Hey!" Timothy said, choking on laughter. "What are you doing?"

"I've decided that when you get worried, I'm going to tickle you to make you smile and forget," Joiner said with a chuckle. "You're welcome to be there, you know that. We just didn't think it was a good use of your time. Besides, if you use up all your vacation time, then you won't have any left, and I was thinking that maybe this winter we could see Mom and Carter for a few days and then maybe take a cruise out of Florida. I know this is important to you, but win or lose, life will go on."

"You're right," Timothy agreed, setting down his mug.

"I usually am," Joiner quipped and jumped back as Timothy took a lighthearted swipe at him. "See, you're smiling. There's a point where you have to trust you've done all you can, and we have. Now it's up to Gerald, and this is what he's good at. Nothing will be decided this morning, so go into work and design the world's best motorcycle. Just promise me that when they build it, you'll give me a ride on one."

Timothy chuckled. "You better believe it. I'd been saving for one for a while, but I needed to buy a car first. If they choose my design, though, the prize is the first cycle off the assembly line."

"We'll have to get licenses," Joiner said, and Timothy saw Joiner's eyes flash with excitement.

"Speak for yourself; I have one already," Timothy quipped, and he got up to put his mug in the sink. "It's sort of a requirement, even if you don't own a bike. But I haven't won yet."

"You will," Joiner said as he pulled him into a hug. "I have faith in you." Joiner kissed him lightly, but Timothy's lips tingled just like they had with those first few and very new kisses. No one had ever had faith in him but Grampy, and to not only hear the words, but to know deep in his heart that they were true, meant the world to Timothy. After sharing a few more kisses, Timothy hurriedly gathered his things and left after saying goodbye. It didn't take him long to get home and change before heading through town to his office.

"MORNING, Tim," Heidi chirped from her desk as he walked in.

"Morning," he answered and set down his case. Booting up his PC, he gathered his things and got to work, knowing it was the only way he was going to keep his mind off what was happening downtown.

Concentrating on his design worked for a while, but Timothy found his mind wandering. "Are things okay?" he heard Heidi ask over the wall.

"Sure, why?" Timothy responded, taking a brief break from the detail he was working on.

"Well," she began, and Timothy saw her head appear above the wall. "You nearly jumped through the ceiling when your phone rang, and I've been asking you a question for the last ten minutes and you kept answering 'uh-huh.' So I thought I should inform you that we're now married and you've agreed to let my mother come live with us."

Timothy sighed rather loudly and rolled his eyes. He had no doubt he'd probably have agreed to anything, the way he'd been concentrating. "I promise I'll tell you all about what's going on when it's over." He saw their supervisor approaching, and they returned to work.

"I wasn't expecting to see you today," Judy said softly. "Is everything all right?"

"Yes," Timothy responded softly, and Judy motioned toward her office. Timothy followed her back, closing the door once they were inside.

"I'm getting a little concerned about all the time you're taking." She put her hand up to stop him from interrupting. "Not that your work has suffered. But you take a lot of time on short notice without offering an explanation, and I'm concerned."

Timothy thought for a few seconds. "It's not that I don't want to talk about it. My lawyer says I shouldn't because of an agreement with the US Attorney. Before you ask, I'm not in any trouble, and I'll explain everything once it's over." He was getting a little tired of saying that, but it was all he could do right now. "I came in this morning to try to get some work done, though I expect to be out the rest of the week. Hopefully this will be over soon, and I'll be back to work on Monday." He certainly hoped he wouldn't have to go through this uncertainty through the weekend.

"I understand," she said, and she pulled a file from behind her desk. "I saw your preliminary designs for the new cycle, and I must say they're really interesting." She spread the papers on the desk, and they talked about the design. She gave him some suggestions and encouragement, and Timothy left her office energized and ready to work. He spent the next hour working hard, and then his phone rang— the butterflies that had settled down inside him turned into an instant swarm.

He saw Joiner's number on his cell phone and answered it quickly. "What's happening?"

Joiner chuckled. "They've worked through the procedures and process, and rather than start the actual process, they broke for lunch, and we'll resume at twelve thirty. Gerald asked if you could be here by then, and he asked you to bring the coin with you."

Timothy looked at the clock. "I'll try. If I'm late, it's because I got held up."

"I'll be sure to tell him," Joiner said. "How are you holding up?"

"I'll be fine once I get there." Until then he was going to be a nervous mess, but there was nothing he could do about that now. "I'll see you in a few hours."

"Love you," Joiner said softly, and Timothy smiled as he disconnected the call. Timothy took a deep breath and went back to work. When it was time to leave, he said goodbye quietly, stopping by Judy's office before leaving the building and hurrying out to his car. He made it to the bank and got into his safe-deposit box, placing the coin and holder in a small bag he'd brought for the purpose. Closing the box, he placed it back in the vault with the bank associate and hurried back out to his car, driving downtown to the federal courthouse. Remembering that he'd have to go through security, Timothy transferred the coin to a secure section of his case and locked it before placing it on the belt. He was getting very nervous carrying the coin around. Once he stepped through security, he saw Carter waiting for him.

Timothy had never been so happy to see a familiar face in his life. "Have they started?" he asked, wondering momentarily if Carter knew about William. He suspected he didn't and decided to keep quiet about it.

"No, but Gerald and Joiner are upstairs, so I volunteered to meet you," Carter explained as they walked. He led Timothy to an elevator, and they rode up to the second floor and then walked down the hallway to where Joiner was waiting. He opened a door and beckoned them into a small room. Gerald stood up and shook his hand.

"Things went pretty well this morning. The US Attorney seemed quite confident, so he agreed to some things that he might not have otherwise allowed. Also, the judge wants to use a more relaxed atmosphere rather than the strict formal procedures of the court. That's in our favor, because as long as we don't push it, we're more likely to be able to stretch what we can present." Gerald sat back down, and Timothy sat as well. Joiner and Carter sat off to the side. "Were you able to get the coin?"

Timothy unlocked his case, fishing out the bag with the coin case in it, and Timothy heard Carter say. "Here, I brought this for you." Carter handed Timothy a felt-lined wooden case. "This will protect it much better."

"Thank you," Timothy said gratefully, smiling at Carter's thoughtfulness. He carefully transferred the coin to the case and handed it to Carter, who seemed astonished. He held the case by the edges as though it were now a holy relic.

"I honestly never thought I would actually get to see one of these, let alone hold it." The look on Carter's face wasn't avarice in any way, but more like he was touching heaven. After staring at the coin front and back, he handed it back to Timothy. "Thank you."

Gerald checked his watch. "We have to be back in a few minutes. Don't say anything unless asked a direct question by the judge or you're put under oath. While we set the basic ground rules, the judge seems to want to do his own thing, and we need to be flexible. My feeling is that this will feel more like arbitration than a trial, but we'll have to see."

"Do you want the coin?" Timothy asked, and Gerald shook his head.

"No. You hang on to that. It's your property, and I want the judge to see it that way as much as possible. When he asks to see it, you show it to him and let no one else touch it. Not even him unless he specifically asks. This is yours, and you wish to protect it." Carter left the room, saying he had phone calls to make, and Gerald cautioned him that he had agreed to confidentiality.

Gerald got up and led them into another room that looked more like a conference room than a courtroom. A large table ran down the middle, with a huge chair at one end. Gerald, Joiner, and Timothy took their places along one side of the table, while the US Attorney sat on the other side. A door opened, and everyone stood while a white-haired man, very distinguished and quite handsome, took his place at the end of the table. Once he'd seated himself, the others did as well.

"I have handled a number of disputes in my career, and I prefer a table to a bench at this point in my life," the judge explained. "For the benefit of Mr. Besch, I am Judge Christopher Hoeppner, retired, and I will be conducting these proceedings. I want to caution everyone that while my style may be informal, the rules of law and evidence still stand. I have read both briefs on the case. Before we get started, I wish to address Mr. Besch." The judge turned to Timothy, and he tried not to squirm in his chair. "Young man, regardless of how this hearing goes, I want you to know that we all appreciate your honesty and integrity in coming forward. We all realize you could have kept quiet and held onto your coin."

"Thank you, Your Honor."

"Would you please show everyone here the item in question, and then we'll get started?" the judge asked, and Timothy removed the coin and its now impressive holder from his bag and held it where the judge could see it. When he reached for it, Timothy gave it to him, but watched every move the judge made as he examined both sides of the coin before returning it to Timothy. "You are satisfied that it's genuine, Mr. Bellows?" the judge asked the US Attorney.

"Yes, Your Honor," he answered.

"Very well, please present your case, keeping in mind that we are all familiar with previous cases and the arguments used."

Mr. Bellows nodded and laid out his case succinctly, which was that only one of the coins had ever been issued, and that the investigation done in the 1940s proved that no 1933 Double Eagles legally left the mint. "The previous trials have confirmed that. While we do not know how Mr. Besch's family came by this coin, neither it nor the others like it, with one publicized and notable exception, were ever issued or monetized and therefore remain the property of the US Government."

"Mr. Young, do you wish to dispute what Mr. Bellows claims?"

"No, Your Honor, but I do wish to highlight one particular facet of his presentation. He said that they do not know how Mr. Besch's family came by their coin. I believe Mr. Besch can enlighten us. I want to ask everyone here for a few minutes of their time. Our case began with a story passed down from Mr. Besch's grandfather to him." Gerald nodded to Timothy, and he looked at Joiner, who smiled broadly.

"Grampy used to tell me lots of stories when I was a kid. But his favorite was about the time his father took him into the Philadelphia Mint," Timothy began, and he told the story the way his grandfather had always told him. How warm the day was, waiting in line, the way everything smelled. He left nothing out.

When he was done, the US Attorney began asking questions. "That story must have been embellished over the years. Did it ever change when your grandfather told it?"

"Not that I remember. Grampy always said you never forget having a root beer float in a real soda parlor, and he always said that the next one he had was his first date with Grammy."

"Is their case a family story rather than facts?" Mr. Bellows asked the judge.

"That's where it begins. We have been able to determine, through weather records, that Philadelphia did indeed experience unseasonable heat on April 13 and 14 of that year. These records have been made available to the US Attorney. We have also uncovered the diary of Joseph Harbinger Sr., Mr. Besch's great-grandfather. While the diary does not mention the 1933 Double Eagle directly"—Gerald opened the diary to the marked page—"'we waited in line for hours at the hands of bureaucracy and government inefficiency. We waited for hours to turn in our gold coins, only to be given more at the bullion window. In this heat, I was sure Joey would melt clean away, so we stuffed them in our pockets and hurried away from the unbearable crush as quickly as possible.' He also goes on to confirm the root beer float detail." Gerald handed the diary to Mr. Bellows so he could examine it. "That diary was found in the attic of Mr. Besch's family home along with one for each year, going on for decades." Gerald waited, and the diary was then handed to the judge, who examined it.

"I know what these are." He opened the front cover and nodded. "My mother used to swear by them. Do you wish to dispute this?"

"No, Your Honor," said the US Attorney, and Timothy saw him looking rather piqued.

"We have one more piece of the puzzle." Gerald reached into his briefcase and pulled out the packet of papers they'd found the previous night. "I must apologize to the US Attorney and to you, Your Honor; these papers were located late last night."

"Why weren't they immediately made available to my office?" the US Attorney asked with relative calm, but Timothy could see he was fuming.

"Because Mr. Besch was confronted last night by his mother's drug dealer, who also happens to be the man who raped him when he was eighteen years old," Gerald replied evenly, and Timothy saw Mr. Bellows go white.

"How is this germane?" Mr. Bellows recovered enough to ask.

"You asked the question," Gerald responded.

"There is no jury to play to in this room, and I'm perfectly able to determine what is and is not germane to this case," the judge said, and Mr. Bellows looked chastised. "Is this true? Remember, Mr. Besch, you're under oath," the judge asked, cutting through everything.

Timothy took a deep breath. "My mother was an addict, and when I was eighteen, she offered me to her dealer in exchange for a fix, and before I knew what was happening," Timothy said, keeping his voice steady, "he acted on that invitation, and I left home a few days later. Last night, that same man came to my home telling me that my mother owed him money and that he was going to take it out of me. I defended myself."

Joiner spoke for the first time. "I was there, Your Honor."

"You defended yourself?" the judge asked.

"Yes, Your Honor, he did," Gerald answered. "Very well, I might add." Timothy looked to Gerald, silently asking him to get off this subject. "I will, of course, give Mr. Bellows time to review the documents. Most of them are strictly relevant to Mr. Besch, but there is one that is particularly on point for these proceedings." Gerald opened the envelope and pulled out an old piece of paper and set it on the table. "This is the receipt from the bullion window at the Philadelphia Mint, made out to Joseph Harbinger Sr."

"This proves nothing except that they turned in bullion for coin," Mr. Bellows countered.

"Mr. Bellows," the judge said evenly, "let me remind you that earlier today you and Mr. Young stipulated to the findings of the earlier court cases regarding these coins."

Mr. Bellows looked confused for an instant, and when the judge stopped speaking, Gerald began, "Those previous cases required that the government prove a right to seize the coins. You said yourself that you do not know where Mr. Besch's family got their coin. I put forward that they got their coin at the Philadelphia Mint bullion window in exchange for raw gold in April of 1933. I further believe that since Mr. Besch's family paid gold for the coin, in fact, it was indeed monetized in 1933 as part of that transaction, and therefore, this coin is not and has not been since April of 1933 the property of the US Government. We can prove a trail, and that given the turmoil and uncertainty at the time, at least one and maybe more of these coins were in fact issued, even if unknowingly, by the US Government." Gerald turned to the judge. "Your Honor, short of a notarized list of coins with their years and amounts issued for a transaction at the mint, there is no possible way to provide more proof than what we've done." Gerald stopped, and the judge looked to Mr. Bellows.

"Would you like to review the documents?" the judge asked Mr. Bellows.

"No, Your Honor."

"Do you have anything to add?" the judge asked, turning to Gerald.

He seemed surprised, and so was Timothy. He'd expected this to drag out for days, but in a few hours Gerald had laid out a case that, if it didn't refute, at least knocked holes in many of the government's arguments.

"The government still maintains that no 1933 Double Eagles were ever issued, and that Mr. Young has only presented circumstantial evidence that in no way proves the origin of the particular coin in question," Mr. Bellows said.

"Thank you both. You have been gentlemen, all of you, and that's very rare these days. I want to especially thank you, Mr. Besch. I have been a coin collector for forty years, and I never thought that I would get to hold a 1933 Double Eagle in my own hands. This case is difficult, and yet it's not. The government has a duty to protect the country's money supply, there's no doubt about that."

Timothy felt his heart begin to sink, and he felt Joiner slide his hand into his under the table.

"However, the government does not have the right to seize property without cause. And in this case, I believe that Mr. Besch has demonstrated that a reasonable doubt exists as to the government's claims that none of these coins were issued. The government's investigation was made almost ten years after the coins were minted, and five years after they were destroyed. It is my finding that the coin in question is a real coin and was issued, knowingly or unknowingly, by the United States Government, and is therefore the property of Mr. Timothy Besch to do with as he pleases. I am ordering the US Government to provide papers certifying the coin's authenticity and validity of the coin within three days." The judge stood, and the rest of them did as well as he exited the room.

Timothy could hardly believe it. He managed to keep himself from jumping up and down. Instead, he reached across the table and shook Mr. Bellows's hand. Joiner did as well. Gerald then stood up and clasped the US Attorney's hand. "A jury would have found the exact same way, Simon. This simply saved a long and expensive trial."

"I'm afraid you're right."

Mr. Bellows left the room, and as soon as the door closed, Timothy clasped Joiner in a hug and began jumping up and down. Joiner held him tightly and actually lifted him off the ground, twirling him around before setting him back on his feet. Timothy felt a little dizzy, and not from Joiner's manhandling. "So that's it?" he asked Gerald.

"That's it. The coin is yours, and you'll get the paperwork from the government in three days. You now own one of only two of them in the world." Gerald patted his shoulder. "It feels a bit anticlimactic, doesn't it?"

"I guess," Timothy answered, and he gathered up his things. He had expected he'd feel relieved and happy that he'd won, and he did, but it didn't thrill him the way he thought it would. He felt the same as he had before the hearing, except without the nerves. "Thank you so much, Gerald, for all your help. I really appreciate it." Timothy gave his friend and lawyer a hug.

"Don't thank me, thank Joiner. He's the one who really did the work. I just guided him through the process." Gerald smiled at Joiner, and after gathering his papers, Gerald left the room. Timothy stared at Joiner. He really didn't know what to say. "Thank you" seemed small and insufficient. Then he saw Joiner's eyes, and Timothy realized he didn't have to say anything at all. Joiner already knew how Timothy felt. He could see it reflected in his expressive eyes. Joiner took his hand, and they left the room together. Carter was sitting in a chair in the hallway, talking quietly on the phone. "They just came out, Sharon," he said and looked expectantly at Timothy, who smiled and nodded. "They won," he said, and he listened before hanging up.

"Congratulations, Timothy," he said, extending his hand and clapping him on the back.

"It was really Joiner and Gerald. They made this happen," Timothy said.

Carter clapped Joiner on the back, and Timothy could see he was proud of him. "Let me take you both to dinner," Carter offered.

"That would be very nice, thank you," Timothy said. "Can we meet at Joiner's in an hour? I have to stop at the bank, and I can meet you there." Everyone was agreeable, and Timothy made sure the now exceedingly valuable coin was secure in his bag before leaving the courthouse. He hurried to the bank, wanting to get the coin under lock and key as soon as possible. At the safe-deposit desk, the woman unlocked the deposit box for him, and Timothy carried it to a private room. Carefully, he pulled out the other coins, setting some of them on the counter. All of them were his Grampy's legacy, and he carefully held a few of them up to the light. Grampy had sacrificed so Timothy wouldn't have to. Putting the coins back in their containers, he placed them in the box along with the Double Eagle, closing the lid. After staring at the gray box for a while, he signaled the woman, and they placed the box back in its home and locked it closed. Timothy looked at the bank of miniature numbered vaults and shook his head before following the attendant out of the area, and after thanking her, Timothy left the bank and drove toward Joiner's house.

Carter's black Rolls was already there, and Joiner pulled up right behind him. Carter's driver opened the back door, and Joiner got inside. Timothy followed, a little excitedly. He'd always wondered what a Rolls-Royce would be like. To say it was plush was an understatement. It was like sitting on the world's most comfortable sofa in the back of a car with half a dance floor in front of him. "I made reservations downtown."

"I'm glad you came," Timothy said.

"I wouldn't have missed it for the world. There have always been rumors that there were some of these coins out there, but no one I've ever met has ever seen one, or admitted that they have, other than the one that was auctioned off a few years ago." Carter settled back, and the driver wound through town, pulling up in front of an impressive building.

"What is this?" Timothy asked, peering out the window.

"The University Club," Carter answered as the door opened. Timothy looked all around as they went inside and were escorted through the awe-inspiring neoclassical building and into the dining room. "They have the best food in town." Talk about fancy… Timothy looked down at his clothes and once again felt a bit like a poor relation. The coffered ceiling soared above them and the subdued lighting and candles made the walls and fabrics shimmer. As they were led to their table, Timothy felt like every eye in the place was on him.

"It's okay," Joiner said with a smile, and he felt him touch his hand lightly. Immediately, Timothy felt better, and when they arrived at their table, Timothy took a seat next to Joiner.

"A bottle of your finest Bollinger," Carter told the maître d', and he nodded and left the table. "Congratulations to both of you."

Timothy picked up the menu and tried to figure out what all the strange dishes were. He'd just settled on the duck when a man arrived with a silver bucket and a bottle of what looked like champagne. He showed it to Carter and then popped the cork, pouring a glass for each of them before quietly leaving the table. "To success for both of you," Carter toasted, and they lifted their glasses and drank.

After they talked a little more, a waiter in a tuxedo appeared at their table, and they placed their orders. In the end, Timothy went with what Joiner was getting. "So how does it feel?" Joiner asked.

"Strange," Timothy answered truthfully. "I keep asking myself if that was it. It seemed like the hearing went by so fast."

"The government's case was known, and the only important thing was what we could present," Joiner explained.

"Have you decided what you want to do with the coin?" Carter asked as he sipped from his glass.

"I think I have," Timothy said, and he turned to Joiner. "When we started all this, I thought having the coin would be like having a part of Grampy, but it's not like that. I have my memories and his stories, and that's the part that's important."

"What are you saying?" Joiner asked.

Timothy turned to Carter. "I'm saying that I'm going to sell the coin."

"I can put you in touch with a very reputable auction house. They've handled this type of thing before."

"That's not what I had in mind. I saw the way you looked at it. So provided we can negotiate a fair price, I'll sell it to you. I know it'll mean a great deal to you, and if I keep it, it'll just sit in my deposit box. Yeah, I'll own it, but it's not like I can really afford to keep it. I'll hang on to the others; that'll be enough," Timothy said, and he saw both Carter and Joiner smile.

"Are you sure about this?" Joiner asked.

"Yes," Timothy answered confidently. He was sure about this, and many other things in his life right now, but he wasn't going to talk about those things in front of Carter. Those particular words were for Joiner alone. Their appetizers arrived, and Timothy settled back in his chair with a smile on his face. Now that he'd made his decision and knew what he wanted to do, he truly felt at ease and happy, regardless of the fancy atmosphere that held more than a hint of snootiness. Timothy ate steak tartare for the first time in his life and found it surprisingly good. His salad was amazing, and the veal entrée melted in his mouth. Dessert, a chocolate and mint tower garnished with a sprayed chocolate silhouette of a spoon on the plate and a cookie spoon, looked amazing and tasted even better. By the time they'd finished, Timothy had had enough wine that he was glad he didn't have to drive.

Carter dropped them at the house, and after saying goodbye, his driver pulled away. "Is he going home?"

"Yes. He'll probably doze off on the way," Joiner said as they stepped inside.

"Does he know about William?" Timothy asked as he turned on the hall light.

"No. I'll tell him when we can talk privately," Joiner said and moved closer. "I don't want to talk or think about him right now."

Timothy's head buzzed slightly, and his body tingled, but more than anything he felt relaxed and happy. Joiner led the way through the apartment, and Timothy followed, walking right into Joiner's bedroom, stripping off his clothes before climbing into bed. "Are you tired?" Joiner asked as he got ready for bed as well.

Timothy didn't answer and waited for Joiner to get into bed before climbing on top of him. He loved how Joiner's skin felt against his, and he squirmed slightly, his cock rubbing along Joiner's. "Are you really sure about what you want to do?" Joiner asked, sliding his hands along Timothy's cheeks.

"Yes. I don't need it anymore. As I said, I have my memories of Grampy, and I have you to love me. I don't need to hold on to things to make me feel special, because you do that every day. I think I was holding on to things that were Grampy's because I needed to remember that someone loved me." Timothy smiled before taking Joiner's lips in a deep kiss, and Joiner wrapped his arms around him in a hug so tight that Timothy knew Joiner was never going to let him go, and that was exactly what he wanted. After years of insecurity, fear, and suppressed pain, he felt whole and loved again. He didn't need things to tell him he'd once been loved because he was loved now by the most wonderful man he'd ever known in his life.

"I love you, my Timothy," Joiner whispered between kisses that curled Timothy's toes and made his cock throb between their bodies.

"Then show me, make love to me," Timothy said. He wasn't totally sure about this. Timothy knew Joiner would never hurt him, that wasn't the issue—he just didn't want to flash back to what had happened to him. Joiner rolled him on the bed, continually kissing until

Joiner pulled his lips away from his, kissing his way down Timothy's skin. Timothy waited more nervously than he liked, wondering how Joiner entering him was going to feel. When Joiner lifted his legs, Timothy tensed and closed his eyes.

"Jesus," Timothy cried as Joiner's tongue skimmed over his hole and then up his balls and cock before sliding down his length. Timothy's legs spread on their own, hips thrusting into the sensation. Joiner continued using his mouth on him, licking and sucking his skin from cockhead to puckered opening. Timothy fisted the bedding, his head rolling as Joiner threatened to blow his mind. On the next pass, Joiner took him deep, sucking hard, and Timothy's eyes crossed, and he felt Joiner work one finger inside him. It didn't hurt, but then he felt Joiner touch something inside him, and a jolt of excitement, like sexual lightning, shot up his spine. "What was that?"

Joiner's eyes smoldered. "That's your body telling you how much I love you." Joiner sucked him down deeply again, and Timothy felt his eyes roll back into his head as Joiner played his body like a fine instrument. Timothy felt his opening stretch, and he hissed, but the discomfort quickly morphed into even more pleasure, especially when Joiner's tongue did this thing around the head of his cock that sent him into near complete orbit. Then Joiner pulled his fingers out of him, and Timothy raised his head, wondering what was going on. He saw Joiner shift between his legs and heard a package open. Joiner reached for the bottle of lube, and Timothy felt Joiner coating him.

Joiner leaned across Timothy's body, kissing him hard, and he felt Joiner press at his entrance and then slowly slide into him. At first the words were on the tip of Timothy's tongue for him to stop, but then everything changed, and Timothy realized Joiner was inside him, connected with him, and the fear and mental pain drained away. "Love you," Joiner said before kissing him hard. Timothy could feel Joiner loving and jumping inside him, and it felt strange and wonderful at the same time. Then, slowly, Joiner pulled away, and Timothy gasped. And as Joiner slowly pressed back inside, Timothy moaned so loudly and long he wondered if he'd ever be able to stop. Thoughts of what had happened before flashed through his mind, but Joiner's care and the way he continually caressed Timothy's skin and expertly stroked his dick banished all thought of anyone and anything but Joiner. As Joiner picked up speed and power, the bed began to rock, and Timothy let loose with an unfettered cry.

"You like that?" Joiner asked, and he did something different, because with his next thrust Timothy saw stars. "You look amazing all laid out for me." Joiner fucked him damned near to oblivion, stroking and loving to the point that by the time Timothy felt his climax build, he could barely see through the joyful tears in his eyes. "Want to watch you," Joiner told him as he damned near pounded him into the mattress, and Timothy arched his back and came with a shout that almost deafened him.

By the time he came back to himself, Joiner was holding him, and Timothy couldn't remember how Joiner had gotten beside him as he tried to catch his breath. "Love you," Timothy gasped as Joiner hugged him close, their legs entwining, bodies pressed together, as happy as he could ever remember being.

*E*PILOGUE

"JOINER, I have something I need to show you," Timothy called as he hurried into the house.

"I'm in the office," came the reply, and Timothy hurried to the extra upstairs bedroom that Joiner used as an office when he was working at home. Six months before, Joiner had moved into Timothy's large house, turning it into their home. Together, they'd redone the kitchen, and the last bathroom was next. They were building a life together that sometimes Timothy could hardly believe. Reaching the top of the stairs, Timothy hurried into the office and practically pulled Joiner out of his chair.

"I have something really special to show you," Timothy explained, and he saw Joiner smile before letting himself be dragged down the stairs.

"What's got you so excited?" Joiner asked, and Timothy opened the front door and pointed. "You got it!" Joiner cried before scooping Timothy into his arms.

"Yup, they gave it to me today, along with two matching helmets," Timothy explained, filled with pride. "They took my picture with it and everything." Timothy's motorcycle design had not only been chosen, but rather than merely incorporating elements of the design, Harley had decided to use it in its entirety, and the end result stood in front of their house. "You ready for a ride?" Timothy was already halfway down the walk before Joiner caught up with him. After putting on their helmets, they climbed on the bike, and Timothy started the powerful engine. Once they were ready, he eased it into traffic.

"Where are we going?" Joiner asked when they stopped at a light.

"I thought we could play video games at the Pink Triangle," Timothy answered, and he felt Joiner squeeze him around the waist. The light changed, and Timothy began moving again, making a few turns.

"If we're playing video games, why are we heading back to the house?" Joiner asked in his ear.

"I forgot something," Timothy explained, and a few minutes later, he pulled down the alley to their garage. "I need my gloves, and I left them in the trunk."

Joiner got off the bike and lifted the garage door. Inside was the exact match for Timothy's bike. "That's number two," Timothy said as he reached into his pocket and pulled out the keys. "Happy anniversary," he added with a grin.

Joiner looked speechless as he stared at the bike. Joiner took off his helmet and walked slowly to where Timothy waited. "I love you," Joiner told him, and Timothy took off his helmet as well.

"I love you too." They kissed right there in the alley, paying no attention to anyone who might be looking. When their kiss broke, Timothy smiled. "It's Thursday, and you know what that means."

"It's Mario Cart night," Joiner said as he walked toward his bike.

"Yup." Timothy pulled on his helmet and waited for Joiner to pull his bike out of the garage and close the door. Joiner got on the bike, and Timothy could see the smile on his face as he started the engine. "Last one there is Princess Peach!"

ANDREW GREY grew up in western Michigan with a father who loved to tell stories and a mother who loved to read them. Since then he has lived throughout the country and traveled throughout the world. He has a master's degree from the University of Wisconsin-Milwaukee and works in information systems for a large corporation. Andrew's hobbies include collecting antiques, gardening, and leaving his dirty dishes anywhere but in the sink (particularly when writing). He considers himself blessed with an accepting family, fantastic friends, and the world's most supportive and loving partner. Andrew currently lives in beautiful historic Carlisle, Pennsylvania.

Visit Andrew's web site at http://www.andrewgreybooks.com and blog at http://andrewgreybooks.livejournal.com/. E-mail him at andrewgrey@comcast.net.

The ART stories

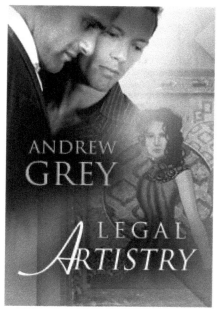

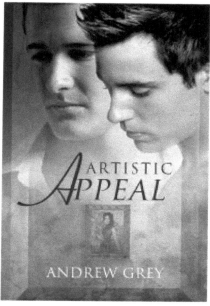

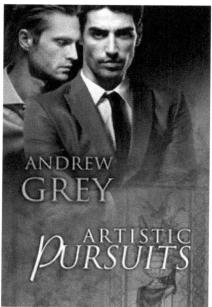

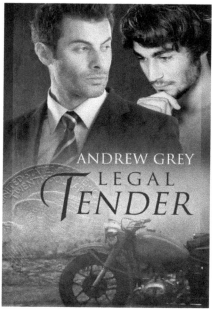

http://www.dreamspinnerpress.com

Now in Spanish, French, Italian, and English

http://www.dreamspinnerpress.com

Also by ANDREW GREY

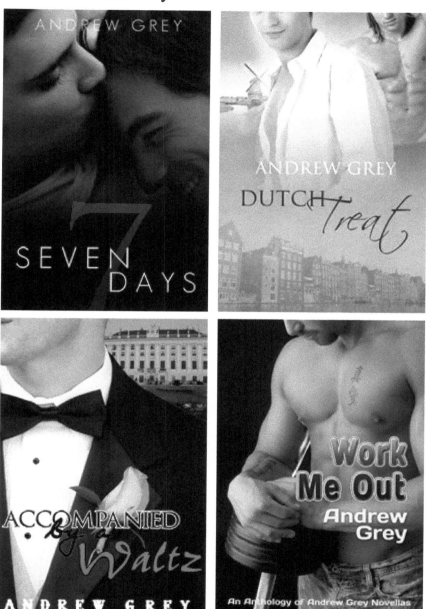

http://www.dreamspinnerpress.com

The LOVE MEANS… stories

http://www.dreamspinnerpress.com

The RANGE stories

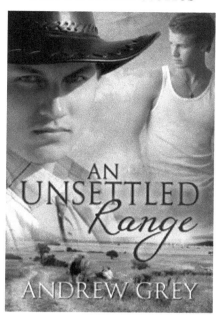

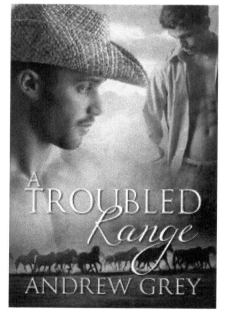

Contemporary Fantasy by ANDREW GREY

Lightning Source UK Ltd.
Milton Keynes UK
UKHW02f0706140918
328884UK00012B/627/P